Tales of the Sacred
and
the Supernatural

Tales of the Sacred and the Supernatural

BY

MIRCEA ELIADE

THE WESTMINSTER PRESS
PHILADELPHIA

Book Design by Dorothy Alden Smith

First edition

Published by The Westminster Press®
Philadelphia, Pennsylvania

PRINTED IN THE UNITED STATES OF AMERICA
9 8 7 6 5 4 3 2 1

Library of Congress Cataloging in Publication Data

Eliade, Mircea, 1907–
Tales of the sacred and the supernatural.

Contents: Les Trois Grâces—With the gypsy girls.
1. Fantastic fiction, Romanian—Translations into English. 2. Fantastic fiction, English—Translations from Romanian. 3. Supernatural—Fiction. I. Title.
PC839.E38A2 1981 859'.334 81-12924
ISBN 0-664-24391-6 AACR2

CONTENTS

FOREWORD— LITERATURE AND FANTASY

THAT which characterizes us as human and defines us vis-à-vis other orders of nature and God is the instinct for transcendence, the craving to be freed from oneself and to pass over into the other, the urgent need to break the iron band of individuality. Dream, the safety valve of this thirst for transcendence, as well as art, magic, dance, and love and mysticism—these all testify from various angles to the fundamental and fated instinct of human nature for emergence from oneself and fusion with the other, for a flight from limited solitariness and a bounding toward perfect freedom in the freedom of the other.

It seems to me that art is nothing other than a magical transcendence of the object, its projection into another dimension, its liberation through magical realization and creativity. This dimension is difficult to specify, but the intuition of it provokes what is called an aesthetic thrill, which is really nothing but a magical joy at the victorious bursting of the iron band.

It is, I say, the joy felt by the one who contemplates it over the fact that someone else, the artist, has succeeded in circumventing human fate, has succeeded in creating. It is the religious thrill of the *creature,* but with this difference: while the creature-feeling which we experience in any religious thrill reveals our dependence on God as one of God's creatures, in the case of the artistic thrill the predominant sentiment is something else: the joy that a *human being* has created, has imitated God's work, has been saved from a destined sterility, has breached those walls of impotence and finitude. On the one hand there is the formula "I am created by God," which inevitably arouses the consciousness of nothingness, of religious fear, of the taste of dust and ashes. On the other hand there is the statement "A human being, like myself, has created, like God," which brings the joy that a fellow creature has imitated creation, has become a demiurge, a force in the creating. That is why one finds so often the spirit of magic in a work of art: it is a projection, through the will and the genius, both magical in nature, of the inner world, the drama of individuality, in a dimension little accessible to the everyday consciousness, but realized and experienced through the artistic act. . . .

The tragic fate, which only a few realize in all its depths, of not being able to go out of yourself except by losing yourself, of not being able to communicate soul to soul (because any communication is illusory, except for love, which is a communion), of remaining terrified and alone in a world which in appearance is so osmotic, so intimate—that tragic fate can only incite an unwearying struggle against itself, an immensely varied combat in opposition to its laws. Hence the magical, artistic impulse of genius which cries that the law is for others, while play and fantasy are for the demon in us, for the artist and the dreamer. We are conditioned by creation and are ourselves created. But that creative and self-revealing instinct transcends creation. We create! We ignore the law and are beyond good and evil. We create through play, and we realize that dimension of dream wherein we enjoy absolute freedom, where the categories of existence are ignored and fate is suppressed. Any revolt against the laws of fate must have the character of play, of the divine. . . .

The magical structure of play and fantasy is obvious. In its "leap" it creates a new space with a centrifugal motion, in the center of which stands, as it were, the demiurge, the creative force of a new cosmos. From it, from this actualization of primordiality, everything begins. This leap *outside* indicates the beginning of a new world. It matters little that this world will find its own new laws quickly, laws over which new others will be unable to pass. It remains a magical, demiurgical creation, just as a work of art is a creation even if, when completed, it falls under the domination of physical, social, economic, or artistic laws.

Since the body of my contributions to the literature of fantasy, my *littérature fantastique,* is available in German, French, Spanish, and other languages, but only fragmentarily accessible to the English reader, I would like to say a few words about it here in addition to the above remarks on creativity which I first set down in my Soliloquies in 1932.*

In the two novelettes which constitute *Tales of the Occult,* among the earliest of my fictional works to appear also in English (1940, and again in 1970), I wanted to relate certain yogic techniques and particularly yogic folklore to a series of events narrated in the literary genre of the mystery story. In both tales a number of important characters were actually real persons: Dr. J. M. Honigberger, still remembered today for his *Thirty-five Years in the East* (1852); John van Manen, the Tibetan scholar; the learned Islamicist Lucian Bogdanof, whom I knew well in Calcutta in 1930-31; and Swami Shivananda, whom I lived near during the six months of my stay in a Himalayan ashram at Rishi Kesh. In addition to these factual references, however, throughout the stories I also carefully introduced a number of imaginary details intended to awaken suspicions in the cautious reader about the authenticity of the yogic "secrets" described. For instance, at a certain moment the life of Dr. Honigberger is radically mythologized, as a glance at any of his biographies

---

**Soliloquii* (Bucharest: Colecţia "Carte cu Semne," 1932), pp. 47-50, translated here by Mac Linscott Ricketts.

will show. Likewise, the region around Serampore, where some of the events take place, is described in such a way as to reveal its status as *mythical* geography. The same is true of some of the yogic techniques depicted: some correspond to real experiences, but others reflect more directly descriptions given in yogic folklore. This mélange of reality and fiction is admirably suited to my central conception as a writer of "camouflage" as a dialectical moment, and in this connection I wish to say once again that any hierophany is a revelation of the sacred *hidden* in a profane object. In *Tales of the Occult,* I used this camouflage in a basically paradoxical manner, for the reader had no means available within the stories to decide whether the reality was hidden in the fiction or the fiction in the reality, both processes being deliberately intermingled.

In these earlier stories I knowingly utilized a number of literary clichés, for my ambition was to follow as closely as possible the popular models of the genre while introducing into the narrative the dialectic of camouflage. But neither of these earlier works, though typically my own, is fully representative of my *littérature fantastique.* In my other stories in the fantastic vein I have set the dialectic of camouflage different tasks, though it would be pointless to give examples here, since it is almost impossible to analyze stylistically the various types of fantastic tales within the confines of a simple résumé. In fact, I even doubt whether such tales can really be summarized, their literary qualities and their mystery residing precisely in the experienced texture of the narrative, as is so clearly the case in "The Three Graces" published here. I can only say that, besides employing different stylistic approaches in succeeding stories, I have repeatedly taken up the themes of *sortie du temps,* or temporal dislocation, and of the alteration or the transmutation of space. Another favorite technique of mine aims at the imperceptibly gradual transmutation of a commonplace setting into a new "world" without, however, losing the proper, everyday, or "natural" structure and qualities of that setting. In my short novel *Şarpele* (The Serpent), written and published in 1937, a rather ordinary picnic in the vicinity of a monastery is transformed unwittingly into a strange ritual after the unexpected appearance of a snake. But the fantastic atmosphere unfolds almost "naturally," and not a single supernatural element intervenes to destroy the familiar world of a depressingly banal group of townspeople enjoying their picnic. The "parallel world" of the fantastic is indistinguishable from the given, ordinary world, but once this other world is discovered by the various characters, it blurs, changes, transforms, or dislocates their lives in different ways.

In "With the Gypsy Girls" a mediocre, absentminded piano teacher pauses by chance one very hot afternoon in front of a curious house, where, upon meeting a young girl, he is lured into seeing "the gypsies." A series of strange incidents and rather childish games follow; but when, a few hours later, the piano teacher leaves the house he gradually discovers that something is wrong—the town, his house, and his acquaintances have all changed. He is told—but he does not believe—that twelve years have passed while he was involved in the innocent, almost meaningless adventures in the house of "the gypsies."

In a somewhat similar way, *The Old Man and the Bureaucrats* (1979) relates the tale of the intrusion of the bizarre personal memories of an old man on the official bureaucratic world. In this story the style becomes a counterpoint to the narrative which depicts the encounter of two different, antagonistic, and yet finally identical mythological worlds. In an attempt to explain himself to the city police, the old man, Fărâmă, becomes involved in writing out a long, rambling, and hopelessly labyrinthian history of his earlier experiences and memories as headmaster of the primary school in Strada Mântuleasa—an account that seems to the officials to be more legend and folklore than history. In the frustrating process of interrogation the two worlds gradually impinge and merge, and the bureaucratic world begins to function fantastically.

In all of these more recent stories, the "fantastic" elements disclose—or, more precisely, create—a series of "parallel worlds" which do not pretend to be "symbols" of something else. Thus, it is fruitless to read into the events and characters of the stories a hidden meaning that may illuminate certain aspects of immediate reality. Each tale creates its own proper universe, and the creation of such imaginary universes through literary means can be compared with mythical processes. For any myth relates a story or tale of a creation, tells how something came into being—the world, life, or animals, man, and social institutions. In this sense, one can speak of certain continuity between myth and literary fiction, since the one as well as the other recounts the creation (or the "revelation") of a universe parallel to the everyday world. Of course, myth has also an exemplary value in traditional or primitive societies, and this is no more true for literary works. One must keep in mind, however, that a literary creation can likewise reveal unexpected and forgotten meanings even to a contemporary, sophisticated reader.

This is not the place to expand such considerations of the function and significance of *littérature fantastique*. I want only to suggest that such types of literary creativity may also constitute authentic instruments of knowledge. The imaginary universes brought to light in it disclose some dimensions of reality that are inaccessible to other intellectual approaches. But certainly, it is not for this reason that most authors write "fantastic" prose. At least, this is not the case for me. But any work of fiction reveals a method aiming at a specific type of knowledge. The methodological implications of *littérature fantastique* are still to be elucidated and systematized. For a historian of religions trying to clarify and improve his own method, this opens an intriguing problem. Actually, the historian of religions, in the same way as the writer of fiction, is constantly confronted with different structures of (sacred and mythological) space, different qualities of time, and more specifically by a considerable number of strange, unfamiliar, and enigmatic worlds of meaning.

MIRCEA ELIADE

University of Chicago

LES TROIS GRÂCES

"IT'S STRANGE he thought of *that*—strange his last words were, *'Les Trois Grâces.'* "

Almost thirty-nine years ago. In fact, thirty-nine lacking three weeks. A few kilometers from Vevey, in the woods. If the dog's barking had not brought him to his senses, he might have passed by without seeing them. Probably he had been trying again—for the nth time—to find something to rhyme. He insisted on preserving the Latin name in its entirety: *Euphorbia moldavica id est impudica*. Startled, he turned his head. A large black dog was advancing toward him across the gravel, and behind the dog, half hidden by tall acacias and pines, were three villas such as he had never seen before. They seemed to be separate, and yet they were connected—but he did not understand *how* they were connected. He stared at them, fascinated, not daring to blink. (Several months after that, Sidonia, scarcely controlling her irritation, had said to him, "I know it's simply a tic, but if only you'd exert a little will power. Pardon me for repeating myself, but for someone who's looking at you—" "But I don't blink all the time," he interrupted her, smiling. "When something interests me—a painting, a landscape, a flower . . . " "I'm not talking about flowers," Sidonia interjected. "That's your profession." Perhaps it was then, in that moment, that he understood. Those words, "that's your profession," were enough. He shrugged.

"Botany, for me, is first of all a passion; in the second place, it's a very precise science. In any event, I assure you, the tic, if it can be so named, does not appertain to me. It appertains neither to the poet nor to the naturalist.")

"Yes, it is strange indeed," agreed Hagi Pavel. "I mean, the fact that he remembered them, of all things, *then*, when . . . " He broke off abruptly, trying to stifle a sigh. Then, in a lower voice, he added, "May God forgive him!" He picked up his glass of wine.

"Les Trois Grâces," Zalomit repeated absently. *"Les Trois Grâces."*

What a dream house! Oh, to be able to work here a whole summer, to do nothing but write! But the dog exasperated him. It was circling around him at a distance of a few meters, barking more and more stridently, not daring to look at him and yet with its head constantly pointed toward him threateningly. He called to it in jest, "Here, doggie!" trying to calm it. Then his eyes fell on the bronze plaque and he read, "Les Trois Grâces." "Of course! Now I understand," he whispered.

"But actually, what does it have to do with?" asked Nicoleanu. "What did he mean?"

Hagi Pavel directed his gaze toward Zalomit and smiled sadly. "Youth," he said. "Memories of youth. From the time when the three of us were students in Switzerland."

He lifted a hand awkwardly to his eyes and began rubbing them. Then, with a sigh, he refilled his glass.

"I discovered them first," began Zalomit, "but on the following Sunday I brought the others along to admire them too. *Les Trois Grâces*. Indeed, no other name suited them. Because, although there were three of them, they constituted a unity, if you understand what I mean. The boys liked them too, naturally, but I myself was purely and simply enamored—by each one individually and by the three together. We went to see them every Sunday. Once the three of us went on a snowy day. The snow was already several hands deep, but the flakes kept falling, and through the trees, after the lights had been lit inside—because it was in January and it became dark quickly—through the trees, it was as though we had suddenly been transported into a Norwegian fairy tale."

"Another time when we went there, it was snowing," Hagi Pavel interrupted. "But it wasn't so beautiful then."

Zalomit shook his head. "No, you're mistaken. We went in the snow only once, on that Sunday in January, in 1929 or '30."

Hagi Pavel looked at him curiously. "In no event could it have been 1929, because I hadn't come to live in Geneva yet. And not in 1930 either, because I spent that winter vacation at home in Romania."

"Perhaps you're not talking about the same thing," intervened Nicoleanu. "After a few years, memories . . . You know."

"But *Les Trois Grâces* are more than memories of youth," Zalomit interrupted. "At least for me. I had published a plaquette of verses, at my own expense, of course—and without any success, I might add. I had worked that summer on another volume, more pretentious. I was quite enthusiastic about Paul Valéry . . . When I discovered them there, hidden beneath the acacias and pines, I said to myself, 'If you could only write here for a whole summer, alone, unbeknown to anyone . . . ' "

Hagi Pavel turned toward the speaker, frowning.

"I found out the architect's name," continued Zalomit, "and I retained it for a long time, maybe ten or fifteen years. But in spite of all my admiration, I forgot it. Just as I've forgotten so many others . . . " He tried to smile.

Hagi Pavel shrugged his shoulders several times. "I don't quite understand what you're referring to," he said.

"At any rate, it's strange that these were his last words," mused Nicoleanu. " '*Les Trois Grâces.*' "

"As strange as can be," Hagi Pavel agreed. "Every one of us had many adventures in our youth. Some of them we've forgotten; of others we remember only half. What could have made Aurelian recollect, of all things, *Les Trois Grasses?* Maybe because, after all these years, we found ourselves together again—we three who were friends during our student years in Geneva. But we had so many other common memories from Switzerland. Why would he have recalled *Les Trois Grasses?* Especially since, properly speaking—as everyone agreed, not just we three but our fellow students —only two of them were actually fat. Yvonne was more or less the size a Swiss girl of twenty-five ought to have been."

Zalomit changed the position of his chair suddenly and crossed his arms on the table. "I believe we're talking about two entirely different things that have nothing to do with each other. I was talking about the three villas near Vevey called *Les Trois Grâces,* to which we hiked several times, once through the snow on a Sunday in January."

"Now that I listen to you," began Hagi Pavel thoughtfully, "I seem to recall some little storybook houses, with dwarves in the yard and a blue artificial pool . . . "

Zalomit made a gesture of weariness. "No, you're confused with some other villas and houses. *Les Trois Grâces* didn't have any dwarves or a pool."

"Perhaps I am confused," said Hagi Pavel. "But I hope you still remember about Yvonne and Henriette and the third girl, whose name escapes me now, with whom we had almost two good years—some of us *very* good years! You—Yvonne pleased you at first, but I don't believe she was ever a great passion of yours."

"Yes, Yvonne . . . Of course I remember her name! But I couldn't tell you what she looked like. As for the other two . . . "

"Henriette was rather stout, but as we said then, the devil's gift; she had that 'come hither!' And smart as a whip. Do you recollect how she'd tease you when the three of us would meet the three of them at the Café des Vosges? First she'd shout to the whole group, *'Vive la Roumanie!'* Then she'd catch your eye and add, *'Vivent les Alliés!'* "

Zalomit shrugged again, smiling sadly, somewhat humiliated. "I'm sorry, awfully sorry, but I don't remember."

"Well, I understand," Hagi Pavel continued. "You were enthusiastic about poetry and flowers. You saw the world differently from the rest of us. Then too, almost forty years have passed."

"But I haven't forgotten the woods near Vevey, nor *Les Trois Grâces,* although, I admit, I hadn't thought about certain events of my youth for twenty-five years."

Abashed, they all fell silent, avoiding one another's eyes. After a while, Hagi Pavel abruptly picked up a second bottle and filled the glasses with great care, as though afraid his hand might tremble.

"Apropos Yvonne," he began. "Do you still remember what Aurelian called the girls at first? He said, *'Deux ou Trois Grasses.'* "

Zalomit looked at him very intently, then smiled. "He couldn't have said that then, because in those years the book by Aldous Huxley, *Two or Three Graces,* hadn't been translated into French. If he said it, it must have been later."

"All right, all right," Nicoleanu interrupted them. "We all know that memory is like all our other functions and faculties: approximate and perishable. But, to get back to the last words of Aurelian Tătaru, what do you believe he meant?"

"God forgive him!" murmured Hagi Pavel. "Perhaps the fact that the three of us were together, that we had met again after so many years, and just here, in the mountains, as in the old days when we climbed Chamonix . . . "

"This part of the Carpathians doesn't exactly resemble the Swiss Alps," Zalomit observed absently. "If he wanted to tell us something, it was probably this: I realize I'm lost, but I'm not afraid of death, and neither should you be. And perhaps he wanted to tell us that death is a fulfillment, an integral perfection of all the higher faculties with which we were endowed. And opening his eyes and seeing us both there beside him, he recalled the perfect harmony of the three villas, separate and yet forming a single architectural body, and he evoked for us this image, *Les Trois Grâces.*"

"Yes, but you're a poet," Hagi Pavel interrupted. "You see things we ordinary people . . . "

Zalomit looked at him deeply for several moments, frowning. Suddenly his face lighted and he smiled.

"If you'd like to know, I'm not a poet any longer. Since that afternoon of July when I first set eyes on *Les Trois Grâces,* I never tried to write another verse. I've remained what I had to be from the beginning: a botanist. No poetics in the world can attain the perfection and significance of the most timid flower."

He rose abruptly and held out his hand.

"And now, please forgive me for leaving. I'm going upstairs to my room to stretch out. I'm tired."

. . .

Hearing steps on the path, he woke up and looked around quickly. At first he did not recognize him with the beret pulled well down on his forehead and the raincoat over his shoulders.

"In other words, you're not asleep," said Nicoleanu, approaching. He sat down beside him on the grass, wrapping the coat around his knees carefully. "Even in the middle of summer the nights here in the mountains are always cold. You should be careful . . . "

"I'm used to it," asserted Zalomit without looking at him. "My area of specialization is the flora of the Carpathians. As much as still remains," he added, mostly to himself.

"You stopped to rest *here,* just a few meters from the place where—"

"What time is it?" Zalomit interrupted, turning suddenly toward him. "I left my watch on the nightstand."

"It couldn't be later than three. The sun rises in an hour."

"So, no more than twelve or thirteen hours have passed. I find it impossible to understand how it happened."

Nicoleanu wrapped his coat about him even tighter, shivering. "Nor do I understand," he said. "When I heard you shouting and arrived on the run just two or three minutes later, I couldn't believe my eyes. Only an inexperienced child from the city climbing in the mountains for the first time, or someone who had suddenly lost consciousness, could have slipped and fallen head over heels for some twenty to twenty-five meters without trying to grab hold of a root or a tuft of tall grass or even a rock."

"Perhaps he did lose consciousness, or maybe he had a heart attack or something else. I believe this will be determined."

"It may be determined," Nicoleanu interjected, "if the autopsy is made in time and by the proper person."

"Had you known him long?" asked Zalomit, turning toward him again.

"I didn't know him well until the last three or four years. Of course, I'd met him several times before. Since we did not have the same speciality, or, more precisely, he no longer had it, we didn't have occasion to meet very often and get acquainted in the years from 1960 to '65."

Nicoleanu prolonged the awkward silence, still trying to adjust his coat. At last he stood up, found the sleeves of the coat, slipped his arms into them, and buttoned it to the top. "When had you stopped seeing him?"

"Of late we'd been meeting rather rarely, at intervals of several years. But we kept in touch, through mutual friends and colleagues. We seldom wrote to each other, because we were both very much caught up in our professional responsibilities. And yet, when he found out from Hagi Pavel that I was coming to Poiana Dornei in the latter half of June, he wrote to me, proposing that we spend a few days together, the three of us, here at the Chalet. But why do you ask?"

Nicoleanu rubbed his hands together awkwardly. "I want to know if you had kept abreast of his investigations—more precisely, with his discoveries of ten or eleven years ago, when many of us, those of us who specialize in medical biology, believed that Dr. Tătaru had discovered, or was on the road to discovering, a treatment for cancer."

"I heard about that a long time ago. And we even discussed it to some extent. Or rather, I questioned him, and he, although paralyzed by his proverbial modesty, admitted to me once that if he were not prevented by circumstances, in two or three years at the most the death rate for cancer would be less than that for tuberculosis or syphilis."

"Yes, this is true. It's been known that someday the problem of cancer will be solved just as the problems of the plague and rabies, for instance, have been solved. But I don't know if Dr. Tătaru went into the details."

"I don't think so. He just said that the experiments were as encouraging as possible."

"Many experiments have been encouraging," Nicoleanu resumed, "and yet they have not led to any results. The experiments of Dr. Tătaru, which fascinated us twelve or thirteen years ago, were of a different order. They presupposed a revolutionary methodology having nothing to do with anything that had been tried up till then in the scientific treatment of cancer. True, as is customary in such situations, the secret had to be kept until such time as positive results could be verified in what some call a minimal series: that is, in at least three to five clinics. And so none of us knew in what his experiments consisted. We did, however, find out something about their methodological presuppositions. And when, in the last two or three years, we began to be close friends, Dr. Tătaru told me something—of course, not everything, but enough that I understand that what we had heard was not rumors, as was maintained later. Because later, it was maintained—"

He interrupted himself, as if afraid to end the sentence, and remained silent for some time, perplexed.

"Anyway, now it can be said," he began abruptly, "because on the one hand Aurelian Tătaru is no more, and on the other hand it would seem—in these matters one never knows for sure what is truth and what is rumor or propaganda—it would seem that similar experiments have taken place in laboratories in Russia and the United States. In brief, the idea Dr. Tătaru had was this: Cancer is provoked by an excessive and anarchical proliferation of the cells of a tissue or an organ. The physiological process is paradoxical, even contradictory. Because the phenomenon of the vertiginous multiplication of cells indicates a positive impulse—namely, the regeneration of the tissue or the organ in question. In itself, the appearance of neoplasm, the massive proliferation of cells, ought to lead to the total regeneration of the tissues, and ultimately to the regeneration—that is, the rejuvenation—of the entire body. But this positive organic impulse is canceled out by the demented rhythm of the proliferation of cells and by the anarchic, chaotic character of the micro- and macro-cellular constructions; one might say we have to do with a tendency of creation suddenly become amnesiacal, a process physiologically 'a-teleologic,' amputated from intentionality, one which 'creates' unconsciously and haphazardly, without aim, without plan, without structure."

"Extraordinary!" exclaimed Zalomit. "Simply extraordinary! How pleased Goethe would be by this interpretation of neoplasm as a chaotic creation devoid of meaning! And if he ever read it, how much Aurelian must have liked Goethe's *Morphology of Plants*! I'll never forgive myself for not insisting, not begging more insistently, that he talk to me about his experiments."

"Perhaps he wouldn't have said any more," Nicoleanu resumed. "He suffered, as I dared to tell him once, from an almost pathological modesty."

"And so, what happened? Because I never heard him speak of discovering the treatment, and never again when we met did he mention anything further about those experiments which were so promising."

Nicoleanu sighed deeply and stretched out his arm

toward the valley, as if he wanted to point to something. Then, changing his mind, he placed his hand dutifully on his knee.

"What happened I don't know very well myself, but he had to break off his experiments when he was named Chief of Staff at the hospital in Giulăşti. Did you meet him, perchance, in that year, about 1960-61?"

Zalomit was thoughtful for a moment. "No. Neither in 1960-61 nor in 1962."

"Those who saw him then observed no bitterness. He laughed silently, as he always laughed. 'What I haven't discovered, others will discover,' he would say. And then he would change the subject."

Of course, it was fatal; I ought to have realized it long ago. With my experience, I ought to have. The project of the Regional Atlas, three monographs ready to go to press, and all that followed: Ursache's smile, the meeting with Catastrofa-Trei-Ierarhi, but especially their silence, when Imaculata-Concepţiune took the floor . . . He felt all his blood rush to his cheeks, and he came to suddenly, turning toward Nicoleanu with his whole body.

"But actually, how did Aurelian think to rectify the process of the proliferation of cells? In what did his experiments consist?"

"So far as I can reconstruct from what I know and what I heard from him, Tătaru hoped to perfect an organic solution or a serum—I can't be more precise—a solution which, when injected into the region where the proliferation had broken out, would produce a phenomenon, as he told us in jest, of 'anamnesis,' of the awakening of the teleological instinct present in every microorganism. Of course, these are only metaphors. What he believed himself to be on the way to discovering was an agent of reconstruction of the organic impulse. Once he said to me, 'Actually, the discovery will be used more in the medicine of rejuvenation than in the cure of cancer. Because,' he said, 'in a generation or two cancer will disappear as a social scourge, but we will have our work cut out for us with the scourge of cellular degeneration and aging.' "

"A phenomenon of anamnesis of the teleological instinct present in every microorganism," Zalomit repeated, pronouncing the words slowly, jerkily. "If he understood that, he understood all." With a quick movement he was on his feet. "I feel as though I'm dreaming. Everything that's happened since yesterday afternoon seems unreal."

"I too," agreed Nicoleanu, rising with some difficulty. "I can't believe he stumbled and slipped twenty to twenty-five meters on the slope, because it's not even a precipice."

"It seems unreal to me," Zalomit continued, bowing his head, "unreal, that after I followed with my eyes for a good while the ambulance bearing the body of Aurelian Tătaru, we returned to the Chalet and Hagi Pavel ordered two bottles of wine. I find it impossible to believe it was *that way,* that *these things* really happened."

. . .

Hagi Pavel wakened him when it seemed he had scarcely fallen asleep.

"Get dressed quickly," he told him. "They've come for the interrogation. *Au fond, mon vieux, nous sommes suspects,"* he added in a whisper.

In the courtyard, the light of the summer morning blinded him. They grouped themselves around a dark young man who was frowning and gesticulating, holding a notebook in his left hand.

"Comrade Professor Filip Zalomit?" he asked. "You arrived the day before yesterday in the evening, in a car from the Laboratory of Botanical Physiology at Poiana Dornei. Dr. Aurelian Tătaru was waiting for you on the terrace, together with Comrade Engineer Hagi Pavel and Comrade Doctor Nicoleanu. Is that correct?"

"Correct," said Zalomit, not daring to look at his companions.

"Then we can leave. And in order to gain time, we'll take the truck."

"Comrade Ciubotariu," Hagi Pavel intervened, "it's very close, not more than a kilometer."

"In order to gain time," repeated Ciubotariu.

After they had alighted from the truck, he coughed several times and began with some solemnity: "So there may be no confusion, I ask you please not to talk among yourselves. I want you to show me how you started on this path yesterday, June 22, at the hour of two or two thirty in the afternoon. You said in your declaration that Dr. Aurelian Tătaru set off ahead quickly, that is, he separated from you. About how many meters ahead?" he asked, turning to Nicoleanu.

"Hard to say exactly. Maybe forty to fifty meters. At any rate, not more than a hundred. But on account of the trees we couldn't see him."

"None of you could see him?" Ciubotariu insisted, shifting his eyes from one to the other.

"No."

"So, then, none of you saw him," he concluded; and moistening his finger, he turned a page of the notebook with care. "Now, so there may be no confusion, show me how you were walking, at what distance from one another. Tell me, Comrade Professor."

"At first, we walked side by side. Then, when the path narrowed, we went single file, one behind the other. For a part of the time I was in front, but then—"

"Pardon me," interrupted Ciubotariu. "Is that the way it was?" he asked, addressing the other two. "Did he walk in front for a while?"

"Quite so," said Hagi Pavel. "I remained a step or two behind him, but soon—maybe after five or six minutes—Filip, Professor Zalomit, who as you know is a botanist, stopped in front of a plant and bent down to look at it more closely. And then I went on ahead of him, followed by Dr. Nicoleanu."

Ciubotariu looked at each of them in turn, questioning them with his eyes.

"Then, let's go," he said. "Walk as nearly as possible the way you were walking yesterday. I'll remain in the rear. And please, no talking among yourselves."

After about ten minutes Nicoleanu left the path. "Yesterday I stopped here, and I told the others not to wait for me. I climbed a little through the trees, approximately there," and he pointed with outstretched arm. "You understand why. I'm both a medical doctor and a biologist," he added, seeing that Ciubotariu was frowning.

"In other words, that is why you were not present."

"I believe that the others weren't present either."

Ciubotariu opened his notebook again. "Right, they weren't either. Or at least so they wrote, each of them, in the declaration. For how long were you alone?"

"Perhaps eight or ten minutes. Then I hurried, in order to catch up."

"Could you see them at a distance?"

"No. As you can understand now, after only two or three minutes no one could be seen. The path bends sharply several times here, and loses itself among the trees."

"Then, let us hurry," said Ciubotariu.

Nicoleanu and Hagi Pavel were waiting silently near the edge of the woods.

"We had arrived here," began Hagi Pavel, "when we heard a suppressed shout and then a sort of muffled noise which I couldn't identify then—a noise caused, perhaps, by the tumbling of the body."

"And then we both set off on the run," added Zalomit.

Ciubotariu passed silently ahead, then signaled them to follow him. Upon reaching the clearing, they walked faster. A hundred meters farther on a soldier was waiting, smoking in a bored way.

"From here I saw him first," said Hagi Pavel, pointing toward the slope. "It seems to me he was moaning, but I'm not sure now. In less than a minute we were both at his side.

We didn't understand what had happened, why he had fallen, but we didn't believe it was too serious. We thought about how we might lift him and transport him on our arms, but when I laid my hand on him he closed his eyes and groaned."

"Is that how it was?" Ciubotariu queried Zalomit. "He groaned?"

"He groaned, but then he opened his eyes and tried to smile. And because we were asking him over and over, 'What happened? How did you fall?' he looked at us with an expression impossible to describe and whispered, very clearly and without any hestitation: *'Les Trois Grâces.'* "

" *'Les Trois Grâces,'* " repeated Ciubotariu. "So you wrote in your declaration. But did he say nothing else—either before or afterward?"

"Nothing. We were both looking at him, expecting him to add something, when I realized he was dead."

"Dead," echoed Hagi Pavel.

"Why were you so sure he was dead?" insisted Ciubotariu.

"We've both been to war," explained Hagi Pavel. "I put my hand on his heart, so, as a final test, because I still couldn't believe he had died."

"Then I arrived," intervened Nicoleanu. "I also put my hand on his heart. There was no room for doubt. He was dead."

Only after getting out of the truck did they discover that the investigation was not over.

"So there may be no confusion," said Ciubotariu, "I'd like you to clear up two or three further details. Let's go inside the station for a moment." The guard opened the door, then drew it shut and left them alone. After indicating some chairs to them, Ciubotariu seated himself at the desk and began to search in his notebook.

"From your written declarations it follows that although you were quite good friends, you met rather seldom as a group. How did it happen, then, that you met now, for the first time in many years, and precisely here, at Şeştina, in a mountain chalet? Comrade Professor Zalomit says that Dr. Tătaru, hearing that he was to be at Poiana Dornei, wrote to him, inviting him to spend several days with him here at the Chalet. I presume you have kept the letter, Comrade Zalomit."

"I hope I've kept it."

Ciubotariu turned his head suddenly toward Hagi Pavel. "And you, Comrade Engineer? You met rather infrequently in Bucureşti, or at least so you have asserted in your written statement."

"It is true that the *three* of us met rather infrequently. For a while I saw Professor Zalomit more often, when we were living in the same neighborhood, in Popa Nan. Dr. Tătaru I met, after many years, only last winter, but I met him several times in a row. We talked then about the complex being planned at Faraoane, exactly 120 kilometers from here, where I was to take up residence on March 15, and Aurelian invited me for the second half of June. He told me at the same time that the three of us would be together again. The project was not very difficult to accomplish, he added, smiling sadly, 'because it so happens that two of us are confirmed bachelors and the third has been divorced for many years.' We were, so to say, available. During summer vacation, we could meet anywhere. All that was necessary was for one of us to make the decision and inform the others in advance."

"It was the same with me," said Nicoleanu. "Dr. Tătaru informed me ahead of time. I'm a widower," he added.

. . .

He heard a voice he did not recognize right outside the door.

"No need—I'll introduce myself."

In the next moment the door opened admitting a middle-aged man, tall, slender, with thin blond hair combed meticulously so as to cover his entire crown. When he approached, he extended his hand.

"Emanuil Albini. Section of Information and Investigation."

He seated himself in front of a long wooden table and let his eyes run without interest over the boxes containing specimens.

"They're vegetable fossils, or traces of fossils," said Zalomit, smiling. "The majority, ferns and conifers of the Paleozoic era."

Albini looked at him curiously, as though endeavoring to guess what intention he was trying to camouflage by his terminology, neither elementary nor scholarly.

"Are you very much interested in it?" he asked, suddenly deciding to set his briefcase down beside him on the floor, leaning it against a leg of the chair.

"Paleobotany?" smiled Zalomit. "Paleobotany interests detective-botanists above all, and I number myself among the poet-botanists. But I'm interested in Carpathian flora, and therefore—"

"Why haven't you published any more verses, Comrade Professor?" Albini interrupted gently.

Embarrassed because he knew he was blushing, Zalomit drew his chair nearer to the table.

"I didn't imagine that after forty years anyone would still remember . . . "

"*Stained Corollas*, by Filip Zalomit. I read it in *liceu*. And I believe that since then I've read it at least five times."

"I can hardly believe it," said Zalomit, still troubled, sensing the blood throbbing in his cheeks. "Verses of adolescence, pallid and anodyne, echoes of Ion Barbu and Valéry . . . "

"And of Dan Botta and others. But they are not pallid, not anodyne. Otherwise I shouldn't have reread them so many times. I kept searching through reviews of the time, but I never came across the name of Filip Zalomit. Perhaps you published under a pseudonym?"

"No. I never published anything else. In fact, I haven't written any more verses since then, since that summer."

"I too wrote some verses," began Albini in a strange, faraway voice. "I wrote and published even in *liceu*. I published under five pseudonyms," he added dreamily. "But I haven't written any verses for a long time now. As you said last week at the Chalet, I've remained what I had to be from the beginning, an investigator."

He looked at him fixedly, deeply, in the eyes, then hurriedly reached into his breast pocket and drew out a package of cigarettes.

"You, I know, don't smoke. But I imagine that the smoke of English cigarettes does not damage vegetable fossils."

"No," said Zalomit, handing him a ceramic saucer. "They're used to it."

Albini laughed briefly, turning the lighter between his fingers.

"But you know, you were not right about *deux ou trois grasses*," he began after lighting the cigarette. "In a letter of January 1930, see what you wrote to Aurelian Tătaru. I have here a photocopy."

He opened the briefcase and took out a dossier with slightly faded edges. "But it's better you read it," he added, holding it out to him.

After a while Zalomit realized he was following the lines without understanding what he was reading. Actually, we're both under suspicion. Only the two of us were present. But I don't need to be afraid. As a matter of fact, I'm not afraid. Fortunately, I'm past sixty, and like any intellectual past sixty, I'm vulnerable. At the first blow, I'll collapse. Infarction, aneurysm, cerebral hemorrhage, and so forth. Fortunately, I'm no longer young. They have no way to force me . . .

"You're convinced, now, that Comrade Engineer Hagi Pavel was right," said Albini at last. "'Memory, that lofty and permanent treachery . . . ' If I were to drop the word 'permanent,' it might figure as the beginning of a poem. 'Memory, that lofty treachery . . . ' "

"Yes," whispered Zalomit, trying to wake himself. "It could . . . it might be a beautiful poem."

"I regret, however," continued Albini, "that I must invalidate both hypotheses, both yours and Engineer Hagi Pavel's. Dr. Tătaru's last words had nothing to do with memories from your student days. They didn't refer either to the three villas at Vevey or to *les trois grasses.*"

"Can that be so?" exclaimed Zalomit. "And yet they were—"

"In Dr. Tătaru's papers," Albini interrupted, "were found precise references. *'Les Trois Grâces'* in this instance were three patients from Brancovici Hospital, where Dr. Tătaru began his experiments with the serum in 1960."

"But then . . . ," began Zalomit excitedly.

"I learned this from Dr. Căpăţână, the surgeon with whom Tătaru was working then, in 1959-60, at Brancovici. And it was confirmed also by other witnesses: Dr. Huţan, Dr. Tătaru's closest collaborator, two male nurses, and Professor Doctor Nedelcu, head of the Oncology Section."

He interrupted himself and looked at Zalomit absently for a few moments, then cast his eyes toward the window.

"According to what I understand from Dr. Nicoleanu," he resumed, "you were not informed about the researches of Aurelian Tătaru. But now you know what they had to do with: a treatment which should have replaced both radiation and surgery. *Should* have replaced them, but the serum had not yet been tested sufficiently and Dr. Tătaru did not dare object to radiation treatments and operations. In April 1960, Professor Doctor Nedelcu isolated in one wing of the hospital three female patients who had recently undergone surgery. He put them, in other words, at the disposition of Dr. Tătaru and his co-workers. Through a happenstance which would not greatly surprise people like us, poets and even former poets, these patients, aged fifty-eight, sixty, and sixty-five, were named—"

He hunted in the file and selected a page.

"They were named Aglae Irimescu, Frusinel Chiperii, and Italia Gâldău. When Dr. Tătaru read the cards he exclaimed, according to Dr. Huţan: *'Les Trois Grâces!* The

Three Graces, Doctor: Aglae, Euphrosyne, and surely, Thalia, because "Italia" is a typographical error.' Parenthetically let me say, it was not an error; the given name of the woman was really Italia. So that we have to do, in fact, with two or three Graces . . . Why aren't you blinking any more, Comrade Professor? Don't harm yourself!"

"It's unbelievable," whispered Zalomit, and he began to rub his eyes.

"Everything that followed seemed unbelievable too," continued Albini. "Because, according to all the reports, the results were as good as they possibly could be. Dr. Huţan stated explicitly that they surpassed the most optimistic expectations. Yet, in spite of this, the treatment was broken off after about three weeks—twenty-two days to be exact. Dr. Tătaru was named Chief of Staff of the hospital in Giulăşti which had just been established."

"But why?" asked Zalomit, lowering his voice and drawing his chair even closer to the table.

Albini extinguished his cigarette slowly in the ceramic saucer. "Because certain men have no imagination. When Marxist thought will agree to the *massive* use of imagination, the revolution will triumph everywhere, from one end of the planet to the other. The interruption of the experiments was due to the lack of imagination of the head man, Professor Docent Doctor Nedelcu, and to a lack of imagination on the part of those who let themselves be influenced by his anxiety. Everyone was afraid that the success of the treatment would provoke a recrudescence of religious obscurantism."

"I don't exactly understand," said Zalomit softly.

"In a report addressed to the Cadres, Professor Nedelcu wrote that Aurelian Tătaru was making jokes, but also allusions, of a religious nature. He even cited examples. For instance, Dr. Tătaru supposedly said once, in a group of doctors, that in Paradise, Adam and Eve were periodically regenerated—that is, rejuvenated—by means of neoplasm; that only after the intrusion of original sin did the human body lose the secret of periodic regeneration and therefore of youth without old age; while from then on, from time to time, by a strange and sudden anamnesis, the body tries to repeat the process, and the blind proliferation of neoplasm produces a malignant tumor."

"But this is only a joke, or perhaps a metaphor!" exclaimed Zalomit.

"Maybe it was not just a joke, but even so, what importance could the metaphors or theological commentaries of Dr. Tătaru have so long as he did not enourage any counterrevolutionary activity? If Professor Nedelcu and the men of the Cadres had had any imagination, they would have understood that the only thing that counted was the scientific results of the serum. But unimaginative men allow themselves to be hypnotized by clichés and slogans. Religious obscurantism!" Albini became suddenly cheerful, as though he had remembered a successful pun. "Of course, magical and religious superstitions are quite dangerous. But even Russian scholars have not hesitated to study yogic and shamanistic practices, while the most important in psychometric and parapsychological research has been realized in Soviet laboratories."

He interrupted his discourse and sought the other man's eyes with a look that was full of meaning.

"We have lost ten years," he resumed after a while. "And the chances of recovering the formula for the serum are minimal. Because after the removal of Dr. Tătaru to Giulăşti, part of the laboratory he had set up at the Medical Faculty passed to another section, reserves of the serum were destroyed, and worst of all, Dr. Huţan, believing his career had been compromised on account of his collaboration with Aurelian Tătaru, burned all his personal notes and switched his area of specialization. For the past ten years he has concerned himself exclusively with pediatrics!"

Again Albini let his gaze wander slowly beyond the window, toward the wooden fence recently painted, and farther, toward the spindling cherry trees with sparse leaves, preserving, seemingly out of pity, a few stunted cherries. He began searching absently for his lighter.

"Nevertheless," ventured Zalomit, breaking the silence which had become unnaturally prolonged, "—nevertheless, it's absurd that for a few jokes, an exceptional savant should be suspected of religious obscurantism."

"It is not a matter of a few jokes. From the reports I read last week, it can be gathered that Dr. Tătaru was indeed interested in theological problems. Or, perhaps, in a certain theological problem, namely . . . "

He paused to light a cigarette.

"This seems hard to believe," Zalomit broke in. "We didn't meet very often, but I never heard him make the slightest allusion to any theological problems."

"So said Dr. Nicoleanu and Engineer Hagi Pavel, as well as several other acquaintances. But in 1960, when he was completing work on the treatment, although some of his statements were so enigmatic that one wonders what he meant . . . "

He opened the file and began looking through it. "For instance, a radiology doctor reported that Tătaru once said: 'I wonder why no one has ever discussed the most convincing argument in favor of the thesis that original sin vitiated the whole of nature, namely, that animals can have cancer.' "

"Still, it's strange he never . . . "

"Probably after his experiments were interrupted he lost interest in theological problems. Just as they don't interest us. Besides, to be perfectly frank, this incident might have been completely forgotten had it not been for several new elements that arose quite recently. First, the information, which seems certain because it has been repeated for the last two years, that in Russia and America similar experiments have taken place, in great secrecy."

"But how do you know they're similar?"

"Because we know at least this much: they don't utilize any of the current therapies and they seek a means of directly controlling the process of the proliferation of cells. In the wake of these indications, several researchers have recalled Dr. Tătaru's experiment and have wanted to know what happened to them—that is, to the *Trois Grâces.*"

"That's something I wanted to ask about myself," whispered Zalomit tensely.

"Against all probabilities, all three operations succeeded perfectly and the patients were cured. At least, they tested negative at the examinations to which they were subjected for six years. But then, beginning in 1967, not one of them came again for checkups. The people at Brancovici say they lost track of them. Actually, recent investigations have established that Italia Gâldău was struck down by a car in 1969 and died in the ambulance on the way to the hospital, and two years later Aglae Irimescu immigrated to the United States, where she had relatives. Nothing has been learned about Frusinel Chiperii, because—and this has been known a long time—Frusinel, or Euphrosyne properly, uses two or even three names. She has been married twice; the first marriage ended in a divorce, but the second man left her. Comrade Euphrosyne changes her identification papers whenever it suits her convenience. Eventually, if she is still alive, we'll find her. But what will we learn from her?"

Silently, with a gloomy air, he opened his briefcase and deposited the file absently.

"In no event will we learn the method by which Dr. Tătaru obtained the serum. This we could learn only through *you,* Comrade Professor." He sought Zalomit's eyes.

"Through me?"

Albini began to laugh with a sudden satisfaction which he made no attempt to hide. "I said, we *could* learn it through you," he repeated. "It's not at all certain. But our only chance, that is, the only chance Romanian science has, is you. Otherwise, why should I have traveled in this heat across half the country in order to find you, hidden here in this village with such a beautiful name but with sick cherry trees half dried up? Why not dispose of them, cut them off at the roots?"

Zalomit shrugged and tried to laugh. "We can't intervene. The fruit trees belong to the collective."

Albini kept staring at him, very intently.

"That's what I want to see," he resumed in a firmer voice. "I want to see you laughing. Because I don't know how long it's been since you stopped blinking. I wonder, will you act like this when some of your colleagues—say Ursache or Catastrofa-Trei-Ierarhi—inform you officially, in writing, that your works have been withdrawn from the printery? Will you forget to blink then also? . . . And, unfortunately so far as you're concerned, it wasn't even a matter of lack of imagination. Pure and simple jealousy—and yet of a lofty essence: academic jealousy, subliminally illustrated by Catastrofa-Trei-Ierarhi and Imaculata-Concepţiune. As for Ursache . . . "

He did not give him time to reply. He picked up the briefcase, set it on his lap, and began to caress it slowly with both hands.

"When Dr. Nicoleanu spoke to you about the methodological step presupposed by Aurelian Tătaru's discovery, you exclaimed enthusiastically, 'How much it would have pleased Goethe!' And you added that Dr. Tătaru ought to have read *The Morphology of Plants.*"

"That's true," whispered Zalomit.

"It's also the only clue we can make use of."

"I don't quite understand how it could be used. What struck me then—"

"It appears to be a joke," Albini interrupted. "But we have to try everything. If only you will reread *The Morphology of Plants*, thinking all the while of the connection you made at Şeştina between the two methods . . . If you just evoke all the images—I repeat, *images*—which the disclosures of Dr. Nicoleanu suggested to you, and if you connect them with the methodological step of Goethe in *The*

Morphology of Plants—You needn't worry about the things you're working on at the paleobotanical laboratory. You've already been granted an indefinite leave of absence from the university for personal research on the contributions of Goethe to botany. You may return to Bucureşti tomorrow. The telegram will come this evening; at the latest, tomorrow before lunch."

He stood up, held out his hand, and headed for the door. But after a few steps he stopped, dug into his upper coat pocket, and took out a calling card.

"This is my personal telephone. As soon as you have something to communicate, important or trivial, call this number. Day or night," he added, smiling, with a trace of sadness in his eyes.

. . .

He rolled over in the bed noisily, as in olden times when, as an adolescent, he wanted to free himself from an image, escape from a thought. He tossed and turned in an effort to stop hearing that whispered command, very close to his ear: "Repeat after me! Repeat after me!" "But who are you?" he had asked. "I'm Calinic," the other whispered. "I knew Dr. Tătaru well. I met him here, several days before you and your friends arrived. Repeat after me, but say it out loud, as loudly as possible: I've heard you're well acquainted with the forest at Crăciuna . . . "

"I've heard you're well acquainted with the forest at Crăciuna," he shouted as if he were addressing a deaf man. "I need a guide. This evening I'll bring you back by car."

There was no one nearby, but when he began shouting someone on the terrace turned his head out of curiosity. Probably we'll both be suspect from now on. Why was there need of such precautions? For twenty meters on either side of the road there was no one. He could have told me in a whisper what he had to say and then gotten into the car.

"I saw you that day too, St. John's Day," Calinic began after the car had started. "I saw you standing beside the ambulance, and then up at the Chalet, on the terrace, but I didn't dare approach you. You weren't alone."

It was strange he hadn't noticed him. How could he have forgotten him so quickly? Even at a distance he looked like an ascetic straight out of a fresco, a disciple of Saint Anthony. When he approached the car, Zalomit realized he was older than he had judged: he might be seventy or seventy-two. His hair had turned white long ago, probably, because now it looked yellow. But his beard was so thin that it made him recall the title of a story read in primary 4: "Lack-beard's Beard." Did he remember this in order to escape from the heat of Calinic's burning eyes—eyes almost monstrously dilated, the color of zinc, deep-set in their sockets, defended by bushy eyebrows rising rebelliously on his forehead? He was so thin that he looked almost tall. His left arm, paralyzed from the shoulder down, hung inert beside his body, as though someone had tried to jerk it off and then had changed his mind.

"There are people who say that this resulted from my stay in the prison, but don't believe it. It was God's will, and he knows what he does; he knows why man has to pass through all kinds of trials. In order to wake up," he added very seriously. "And so it was that I woke up, this very day, before dawn. Today the friend of Dr. Aurelian Tătaru is arriving, I said to myself, as though I were telling someone else. And so I had time to reach the Chalet," he added after a pause. "Because I live beyond the mountains, at a sheepfold. I don't know how Dr. Tătaru found out, but he came to see me . . . Now, take the road to the left. It's a bad road, but it soon comes out into a clearing, and we can talk there without fear. No one will hear us."

Nevertheless, as soon as they stepped out of the car, Calinic began to search the surroundings with his eyes.

"I believe it would be well to have a few wild plants, roots and all, and maybe a flower or two, here on the grass in front of us. If someone should come unexpectedly, I'll pretend I'm telling you beliefs and heresies about them."

He turned over in bed again, in vain. The words kept coming, more and more clearly, repeating themselves twice, three times, before he could suppress them. "Beliefs and heresies, beliefs and heresies . . . About these Dr. Tătaru kept asking me. 'Father Calinic,' he began.—I was formerly a monk. In fact, I'm still a monk, although since my release from prison I'm no longer worthy to go to a monastery. For a while I worked on the embankment for the railroad line in Almaş. Then, when my arm was no use to me at all any more, they pensioned me—'Father Calinic,' he said . . . "

"Did you know him well?"

"In the years 1958 to '60, I knew him very well. He came to see me at least once a month. I was living then at Schitul Antim."

"Why did he visit you?"

Calinic did not reply immediately. He took a campanula in his hand and pointed to it sadly.

"Look at it, how it withers!" he whispered. "How many sins we commit to defend ourselves from the wickedness of men! If you'll allow me," he added, "I'll tell you the whole story from the beginning. I took my doctorate at the Protestant Faculty of Theology in Strasbourg. I tell you this so you'll understand why, one day, Dr. Tătaru sought me out at Schitul Antim."

In that moment it seemed that his voice and vocabulary, as well as his way of behaving, his physical presence, changed in some mysterious manner.

"Several years afterward, I published my doctoral thesis about the Old Testament Apocrypha. 'Father,' he said to me, 'I have a great favor to ask of you. I read your book and afterward I read the whole apocryphal book of Adam and Eve, but I'm not sure you've said all that you know.' I looked at him with surprise, and the doctor began to laugh. 'Don't misunderstand me,' he added. 'From the book I learned one thing: that in the Apocrypha, as well as in certain heresies, there survive, in camouflaged form, many fundamental truths. They survive because they were ciphered in a secret, esoteric code.' 'Did I say that?' I asked him. 'No, you didn't say that explicitly, and that's why I've come—in order to find out more.' 'I must confess,' I interrupted him again, 'that the Old Testament Apocrypha hasn't interested me for a long time. I'm no longer interested in scholarly matters, but only theology and mysticism. That's why I chose to become a monk.' The doctor seemed somewhat disappointed. 'But you still know Hebrew and Greek,' he said. 'I'm not interested in scholarship *per se* either; only in the theology of the Apocrypha. But I don't know Greek or Hebrew, and above all, I'm not trained theologically.' And because I was silent, pensive, he added: 'This is a very serious and very important matter, Father. You theologians content yourselves with the theology of original sin, but for me it's a question of something else, something more grave and complex: it's a question of the biological and medical implications of the doctrine of original sin.' He stopped speaking all of a sudden and started pacing the floor. 'Because we know today, Father, that God did not wish to, or could not, destroy his own creation. Man has remained the *same*, the way Adam and Eve were in Paradise before sinning. The same—that is, endowed with the same biological potentialities. In the human body *everything* has been preserved, Father, including therefore the secret of eternal life with which Adam had been gifted.' "

Desperate, he turned over again in bed and covered his ear with the pillow.

"Listen to me, *domnule* Professor," he had said, all of a sudden raising his voice, "listen closely because we won't have a chance again to talk so peacefully, undisturbed by anyone." He pressed the pillow down with fury, but he kept hearing: "Listen to me, *domnule* Professor!" When Calinic's voice awakened him, he realized that for some time he had not been listening. He had been trying to remember whether or not Albini had suggested that he stop at the Chalet on the road to Bucureşti. "Forgive me, Father

Calinic, but I suddenly remembered something, something to do with Dr. Tătaru, a very important matter, and I didn't dare interrupt you. You were saying that everything has been preserved in the human body." "That's what Dr. Tătaru said, and he repeated it to me several times, on various occasions. Because, strange as it may seem, we became friends and the doctor visited me frequently. And he kept returning to his axiom: that God did not abolish definitively the *system* ciphered in the structure of the body and human life. This system, he said, entails rejuvenation and life indefinitely prolonged; it entails them for the simple reason that it is a system of self-regeneration as well as self-regulation. The original sin could not destroy the mechanism of regeneration, but only modify it in such a way that it can no longer be recognized. Moreover, it camouflaged it in certain physiological processes which apparently indicate that exact opposite of regeneration—it camouflaged it in certain maladies and especially in the most dangerous organic disease, the proliferation of cells, neoplasm."

"Yes, I've heard about this also. Though I didn't hear it from him, Aurelian Tătaru, but more recently, since the accident. It was Dr. Nicoleanu who told me first. Still, I don't understand what connection all these things have with the Apocrypha of the Old Testament, with the apocryphal Life of Adam and Eve."

"I had begun to tell you, when I saw that although you were looking deeply into my eyes without blinking, your mind was not on what I was saying. The connection was this: the doctor believed that certain fragments of the original revelation had been preserved in a degraded, mutilated form in apocryphal books. And he wanted to find out from me if there were not perhaps some key with the aid of which we could decipher these revelations hidden and forgotten for millennia. For instance, he wondered if in the apocryphal Life of Adam and Eve there are allusions to illnesses which they and their offspring suffered after their banishment from Eden."

He broke off abruptly and looked him in the eyes for several moments, hesitating.

"Go on, Father. I'm listening."

"I know, but I'm wondering if I have the right to say more. I've told these things to no one but my father confessor, and he gave me dispensation to repeat them when different times should come, and when I should meet persons prepared to understand them. But I'm an old man, and if I don't tell them to you who were his friend, everything I disclosed to Dr. Tătaru ten or eleven years ago will perish with me. He didn't dare communicate them to anyone else, because he didn't know and didn't want to know another theologian."

He fell silent again, lost in thought.

"If you believe it better to preserve the secret, I do not insist . . . "

"No. You, a man of science and his friend from youth—you ought to know. I shall say them to you as they were imprinted on my mind after many prolonged discussions with Dr. Tătaru. He had arrived at an entirely original conception of disease. For Dr. Tătaru, diseases constituted our only chance of recovering what our first parents, Adam and Eve, lost—that is, youthfulness without aging and a life without precise limits. That was the reason why he wanted to learn from me what the Old Testament apocryphal books say about the origin and significance of disease. He confessed, however, that he had not succeeded in understanding the *theology* implied by the meaning he had discovered: *why*, he kept asking me, why is it that, although very soon all cancer patients not only will be cured but will regenerate and rejuvenate, why will a great many years pass before medical biology succeeds in identifying the process of periodic regeneration and rejuvenation applicable to healthy men? . . . Do you understand what he was referring to?"

"I believe I understand part of it. For the time being, neoplasm constitutes our only chance of rejuvenation. And to him, perhaps this seemed unjust."

"I never heard him speak of injustice. He said, however, that he was troubled by the theological mystery hidden in this fact: only someone threatened by the most grave danger—only he, for the time being, has a chance of obtaining youth without old age."

"—and life without death," he found himself adding, half in jest.

"This I don't dare think about—life without death. But he asked me, can theological thought accept this conclusion: that the dialectic of Creation itself calls for the process of regeneration to begin only when the organism is threatened by death? And sometimes he was tempted by heretical thoughts. He said once, 'Just as Luther urged us to sin—*pecca fortiter!*—because only this way will we be saved . . .' But I interrupted him. 'Stop there, Doctor! The sin of pride is threatening you.'"

"Pardon me for interrupting, but I don't understand how Aurelian Tătaru, an eminent medical doctor, ever became so enthusiastic over theology."

"I didn't understand it either at first, and I asked him one day. 'Out of desperation, Father,' he replied. 'I became a theologian out of desperation. I couldn't succeed in integrating the presuppositions and conclusions of my discoveries into any other system. Because, for me, there is no longer any room for doubt: the proliferation of cells represented, originally, a process of regeneration blocked subsequently by amnesia. Such a phenomenon is impossible to explain unless we presuppose a catastrophic mutation in the biological history of man. But when could this have been produced? Only at the very beginning, because all the fossil skeletons that have been found prove that the first men knew, just as we do, disease and old age. Therefore, the mutation took place in the era—mythic or not, it matters little; I, as a man of science, do not let myself be impressed by words—it took place in the era immediately following the banishment from Paradise. The punishment of which the third chapter of Genesis speaks was this: amnesia. The human body simply forgot that it had been endowed with an essential function: the autoregeneration of the cells.' "

Suddenly reaching a decision, he jumped out of bed and turned on the lamp. 2:25. Useless to try. I won't go to sleep until dawn. Better to write now, at random, whatever comes into my head. He began to dress rapidly, because he felt the chill of the room taking hold of him. Sitting on the edge of the bed, he placed the notebook on his lap. I must begin with this, with what Aurelian said about amnesia. But after he had written a few hasty lines, he stopped, frowning. There was something else about amnesia, something very interesting; although he said it in another context . . . "Yes, the Tower of Babel, Father Calinic, is the clearest expression of amnesia. Those men undertook a work—ambitious, absurd, sacrilegious, whatever you wish to call it—but they knew what they wanted to do. They wanted to build a tower that would reach to heaven. God intervened in a very simple way: he provoked a mutation, this time of a mental order. He confused their language. No longer did they understand one another, no longer could they communicate. Their goal, even if they had not forgotten it, could no longer be attained, because the activity of those thousands of men had become now a chaotic agitation, without purpose, like a gigantic, monstrous proliferation of cells."

He wrote: Babel, the clearest expression of amnesia. But then he changed his mind about writing. It would be simpler to dictate into a machine at the office tomorrow or the day after. Just then he realized that Father Calinic had not spoken at all about his meeting with Aurelian Tătaru two or three days before the accident. He sprang to his feet in alarm. I'll have to go back tomorrow morning to look for him. But how had he failed to ask him? They had spent some two hours in the clearing talking. Just about the importance of diseases. Because, said Dr. Tătaru, only in exceptional cases can you discover the germs of healing—when just then they saw a group of hikers coming down from the Chalet.

"The legend of this flower is quite beautiful," he began. "I've heard it from several . . . "

Some of the vacationers stopped to listen.

"But now, we ought to be going," said Calinic, concluding the story, "if we want to reach Crăciuna while there's plenty of light."

In the car he recalled suddenly how much satisfaction it had given him to open the telegram from Bucureşti. He had read it several times, then had headed for the laboratory to inform his superior. "The most important days in the life of a naturalist are . . . ," as Linnaeus said. But was it really Linnaeus who said it? —"The most important days in the life of a naturalist are . . . " "I'm listening to you, Father," he said, coming to his senses and realizing that the old man had been silent for a long time and was holding his paralyzed arm on his lap with his right hand.

"You haven't been listening to me for quite a while, *Dle* Professor. And it's not necessary we talk now, while the road's so difficult. We'll continue when we come out of the woods."

But at the edge of the woods they had come upon a young couple; the girl had sprained her ankle and was biting her lip to keep from crying. He took them to the village, where they had lodged the previous night. But before they reached the town, Calinic had gotten out of the car. "It's only a little way from here," he said, pressing Zalomit's hands, looking warmly and deeply into his eyes. Perhaps he told me about his reunion with Aurelian when I wasn't listening, when I was thinking about the telegram and Linnaeus. But I'll ask his pardon. He won't be hard to find. "I live beyond the mountains, at a sheepfold." Father, I will say, forgive me! Tomorrow, when we have our talk . . .

. . .

He could not bear to withdraw from the window. *Outside 'tis snowing peacefully, within the fire is burning* . . . Between the ages of six and eleven, one cannot speak very beautifully. It is as correct as possible, and it's even poetic: *Outside 'tis snowing peacefully* . . . Ah! the curtain of flakes seems to tremble, to shiver perhaps in anticipation of the wind. Or perhaps not. December 21, 22, and 23. Three days. And the third day, whatever he might do, whatever he might attempt, will be a lost day. Sidonia had invited him for that date. Sidonia: she was, is, and will be; always the same. For thirty-five years at two- or three-year intervals she had sent him invitations to visit on major occasions. Thursday, December 22, the wedding of Isidora, her only daughter; her third marriage. I can't refuse.

He awakened, hearing the doorbell, and suddenly alarmed he headed hastily for the door. On the threshold stood a smiling old woman, dressed in an overcoat the color of gray plums, with a wool kerchief on her head.

"I beg your pardon," she said, wiping away the last flakes of snow with her hand, "but not until today did I find out what your address was."

She took off her kerchief and shook it several times. Her hair, too black, accentuated even more stridently the signs of old age at her temples and cheeks. She entered, stepping timidly on the carpet.

"I recognize you immediately. You're *Domnul* Professor Zalomit. I saw you last summer, running with the other gentlemen, so fast I thought you'd break your neck before you got to him. *Dle* Professor," she cried, suddenly bursting into sobs, "I killed him! Without meaning to, I swear by the holy cross, without meaning to! Through stupidity, through folly—but I killed him!"

"Sit down in this armchair," he said in an unsure voice, shaken. "Calm yourself. It can't be true. Dr. Tătaru lost consciousness and fell down."

She was weeping, hiding her face in her kerchief.

"I'll bring you a glass of water," he volunteered, starting for the kitchen.

When he returned he found her with her hands placed dutifully in her lap, gazing toward the window. She drank several swallows, then sighed, thanked him, and handed him the glass.

"Perhaps you suspect who I am," she began. "I'm Frusinel Mincu. Dr. Tătaru took care of me."

"Go on," whispered Zalomit, seating himself opposite her on the sofa.

"He treated me after the operation. There were only three of us. We each had a room, and they treated us like princesses."

"The Three Graces," murmured Zalomit.

"He, Dr. Tătaru, called us Amazons." She sought her handkerchief and wiped her eyes.

"Continue," Zalomit urged. "I was a good friend of his."

"Maybe he called us that, Amazons, because he began the treatment and he prepared us, each one separately. He prepared us for the miracle that was going to happen. He did it so we wouldn't be scared. And above all, so we'd be prepared. Because, he told us, everyone would envy us; why us, of all people—poor old women who had had grave illnesses and had been operated on. Why us of all people?"

She turned and smiled at him, her eyes filled with tears. He was surprised by the soundness and beauty of her teeth. There was no doubt they were her own, because when she was smiling he saw that two canines were missing, one on each side.

"*Dle* Professor, if you don't mind, may I smoke?"

"Of course, of course," he said with some effort because his mouth was dry. After swallowing several times, he added, "There, there beside you, you have an ashtray."

She lit a cigarette and after she had drawn deeply the first smoke, she sighed again.

"He called us Amazons in order to prepare us. Because, he said, some time would pass before his treatment would be useful also for healthy people."

"His treatment," Zalomit interrupted, "it was a sort of serum, wasn't it? He injected it in the vein—or how?"

"They gave us shots twice a day: in the morning on an

empty stomach and toward evening, when it was beginning to get dark. His helper, Dr. Huţan, gave them, but Dr. Tătaru was always present. And before lunch a nurse came to take blood. Dr. Tătaru watched her take it, and when the nurse left, he came to the bed with a half-filled glass and offered it to me, smiling."

"What was it?" asked Zalomit, much excited. "What taste did it have? What color?"

"It didn't have any taste. It seemed like a kind of water, rather salty. And as for the color, it just looked like water. Maybe it was distilled water. Although he, Dr. Tătaru, told me one day: 'It's well water. But' "—and she began to laugh silently, seemingly happy—" 'but it's from a fountain.' He said the name, but I didn't understand him very well and I've forgotten it."

"La Fontaine de Jouvence?"

"Something like that. But I'm not sure any more."

"Did he bring it with him, or was it there, on the table somewhere?"

"I can't say. Because when the nurse would take my blood, I'd turn my head toward the wall. I couldn't look at the blood. It made me ill."

"Speak on," Zalomit urged. "What happened after that? What else did he say?"

"Yes, that's what I started to tell you. How he tried to prepare us. Then, he came one morning and although he tried to laugh, I realized immediately he was depressed, it was black in his soul. 'Euphrosyne,' he began, because he said this was my true name, 'Euphrosyne, there's been an order from higher up to interrupt the treatment. But don't worry. The operation and all that followed has cured you. Only . . . ' and I saw he was in a quandary as to whether to tell me or not. But at last he made up his mind and told me—because he wanted to enlighten me and prepare me. He bound me first, with an oath, to keep everything he told me strictly secret. 'Like a holy mystery,' he said, 'as they sing at Christmas: "The star rises up, like a holy mystery." ' "

She bent her head and pressed the handkerchief to her eyes.

"Go on," whispered Zalomit, "go on farther. We were good friends, ever since we were students abroad."

"I swore. And even if he hadn't asked me, I still would have kept it secret, like a mystery. 'Euphrosyne,' he said, 'my treatment is good, but I interrupted it in the middle. That is, what I began has been left half finished. I'm telling you this so you will know and won't be frightened: you, the three Amazons, will live from now on like the flowers, according to the sun.' "

"I don't understand," said Zalomit in a whisper.

"I didn't understand it myself for a long time; I didn't really understand what he meant. But when I returned home, everyone marveled. They marveled at how young I seemed. I was past sixty, *Dle* Professor, past sixty, and yet I looked at the most forty. I lived well, like a princess, I told them. That year I didn't realize very well what was happening to me. Especially since, as fall approached, people got used to me, while in the fall, when I went back to work, and especially in the winter, I looked quite as old as when I entered the hospital. But in March . . . Do you mind if I light another cigarette?"

"Of course not, of course not."

Her hand trembled slightly, holding the burning lighter.

"In March I began—how to tell you?—I began to feel different. I seemed to be getting younger, and all the world was mine. You won't believe me, *Dle* Professor, but my voice changed. I sang like a young woman, and the neighbors crossed themselves. And, you won't believe this either, but I grew younger with each passing month as summer approached. I became young in both body and heart. Pardon my expression, but one day when I looked at myself from head to toe naked, I couldn't believe my eyes. I didn't look more than thirty-five or forty! Then I understood what Dr. Tătaru meant when he said we'd live like the flowers, according to the sun. I got scared. What if people found out? I became ashamed of myself, I, an old woman, as if I'd been changed into one of *those*—you know, old people who want to look young. So I began to hide myself—to hide my youthfulness, I mean. The fairy tale, Cinderella—I liked it very much when I read it in school. If a cute girl like her, seventeen or eighteen years old, could hide her youth and beauty, why couldn't I? I combed my hair any which way, I coated my face with a kind of ointment that looked dirty. But I was afraid. And because I had a chance to come to Bucureşti for three days with the Women's Congress, I hunted up Dr. Tătaru."

"Yes, yes, go on!" whispered Zalomit, very excited. "It was certainly a surprise for him."

"Afterward, I was very sorry I had looked him up, because never had I seen him so furious."

"Furious?" asked Zalomit. "You mean he was angry that you had come to see him?"

"He spit fire! 'Euphrosyne,' he said, 'don't ever try to see me again! It'll be bad for both of us. There are orders from above. The treatment has been prohibited, and if it's learned we met again, we'll both end up in jail!' "

"Perhaps he exaggerated," suggested Zalomit.

"He exaggerated in order to scare me. But he seemed frightened too. He didn't want to listen to me. He repeated what he had told me at the hospital—not to worry, that I was fully cured."

"Didn't he wonder at the change? I mean, the fact that you looked so much younger?"

"He didn't have time to get a good look at me. Then too, it was fall, and I didn't look thirty-five to forty any more."

"And yet, I've been told, all three of you came regularly for checkups to the Brancovici Hospital for five or six years."

The woman smiled again dreamily and straightened a lock of hair that had fallen over her forehead. "I never met the other two again. But we came for the checkups only in winter, a little before the holidays, in the middle of December."

Her face clouded suddenly, and without asking permission she lighted a third cigarette.

"But as the years passed, the harder it became . . . *Dle* Professor, don't laugh at me, don't think I'm a fool, when you hear what you are going to hear. I confess to you as to a priest. So you will understand what happened." She sighed and bowed her head, keeping her eyes focused on a corner of the rug.

"As the years passed, it got harder and harder to hide my youth. You understand what I mean. I was good-looking in my time, and men liked me. I had my share of them, both in marriage and outside, as it suited me. And when summer approached, by the end of May, I didn't know what to do. Forgive me for saying this, an old woman, but I couldn't sleep. I couldn't keep busy in the house or yard, I couldn't think of anything but men. Then I kicked over the traces. I would leave home telling the neighbors I was going to some relative's, and come back after three or four weeks—on other occasions, after three months, as it suited me. Because now I didn't have to work any more, and I had some money put aside. I'd stop somewhere, in a secluded place, change my dress, comb my hair, clean the dust and ointment off my face, and climb aboard a bus or train. Soon I'd make acquaintances, and, to tell the truth, by the second day I'd know whom I was going to sleep with. Lord forgive me, but it wasn't my fault. That's the way God made me, fickle and beautiful, as my second husband used to say, and that's why he left me and ran off into the wide world."

She smoked hungrily, without raising her head, her gaze fixed upon the carpet.

"It was like that again last summer. I spent two weeks at the shipyards in Potcoava, but some men quarreled on account of me one evening, because the one I was living with found out . . . The quarrel turned into a brawl and one man drew a knife, but the others jumped. I was scared and slipped outside before anyone got wind of it. The house where I was staying was right next door. I took my things, what little I had, and ran away."

She crushed her cigarette without looking up and sighed.

"Go on, go on!" whispered Zalomit.

"So I arrived at Şeştina. You'll say I'm a crazy fool. You won't believe me. But, *Dle* Professor, the evening before the accident I met a young man, and I pleased him a lot. I spent that night at his place. He was a mechanic, working at the Chalet. In the morning before he left for work, he told me where we could meet in the woods at about 12:00 to 12:30. We met and we stayed there together, bedded down in the grass, for almost two hours. Then he went back to his job. But I couldn't bear to put my dress and my other clothes back on. You remember, it was a very warm day. I walked around naked like a crazy woman, hair disheveled, dress crumpled up in my hand. All at once I came to and caught sight of Dr. Tătaru, just a few steps in front of me! He was as white as chalk. 'Is it true, Euphrosyne?' he asked me.

"By his gestures I knew he couldn't believe his eyes. 'It's true, *Dle* Doctor,' I replied, looking at him fondly, because I was happy.

" 'Is it true you're almost seventy?' he asked.

" 'I will be in February, *Dle* Doctor,' I answered, and began to laugh.

"I laughed with my hair over my shoulders. I looked him in the eyes, and without realizing it I moved closer and closer to him. God took away my senses. I don't know what went through my mind then. To find him, to give him pleasure—Dr. Tătaru, because he had worked a miracle. I kept laughing as I approached him, and he drew back, frightened, not realizing he had reached the edge of the incline, while I didn't see it—God had taken away my senses. All at once I saw him lose his balance . . . and then he tumbled into the valley! I screamed, but I put my hand over my mouth quickly, because I thought I heard a man's voice; and I crept back to the love nest as fast as I could. The tears started. I wept for shame. I didn't suppose he was dead. I got dressed and returned to Dumitru, the man I'd been with. He told me . . ."

. . .

He followed her with his eyes through the snow until she crossed the street and was lost to sight around the corner. "I'll come again in the summer to convince you I didn't lie." He pressed his forehead against the windowpane, exhausted from sadness. If you come next summer, Euphrosyne, you won't find me. My scientific curiosity is not unlimited, whereas theology and its problems frighten me. I shall present you to the Section of Information and Investigation.

He moved absently away from the window, turned on the lamp, and sat down at his desk. Now we know—that is, more precisely, *I* know—what happened. It wasn't, properly speaking, a suicide. But then what was it? He opened a drawer, found the calling card, and after a brief hesitation picked up the receiver. A secretary answered.

"Who's calling?"

Upon hearing the name, she replied in a frightened voice, "Wait just a moment!"

He did not wait long. There came a voice, unctuous and polite, of a young man. "*Dle* Professor Zalomit? Comrade Colonel left ten minutes ago. He was headed for your place. He ought to arrive any moment."

He replaced the receiver very carefully because his hand was shaking; then he remained immobile, waiting for the pounding of his heart to subside. When the doorbell rang, he ran his hand through his hair several times, preparing a smile and a suitable look of surprise, and went to open the door.

"What a coincidence!" he exclaimed.

"Isn't it!" said Albini.

And as soon as he had hung his coat on a hook, he headed straight for the desk, lifted the receiver, and manipulating skillfully the blade of a knife he removed a few screws.

"We won't be needing that from here on," he said.

"In other words . . ., " began Zalomit, forcing himself to smile again.

"I had recourse to this strictly technical detail in order to simplify your mission. The conversation, or rather the confession, was recorded on tape. You will receive the text typed in a day or two. But isn't it truly extraordinary? Were you expecting something of the sort?"

Zalomit ran his fingers through his hair several times, irritated that he could not control the trembling of his hands.

"I confess, frankly," Albini continued, "I wasn't prepared for it." He took out a package of cigarettes. His eyes fell on the ashtray half filled. "Musn't forget that detail. Always offer her cigarettes, and good ones too!"

He turned his head abruptly and sought Zalomit's eyes. "You sound wrought up, *domnule* Professor, and I understand very well. We were expecting everything, but the attempted seduction, the result of the treatment . . ."

"No! I wasn't thinking about that," Zalomit began in a firm voice. "I was wondering if it was a suicide. As well as I knew Aurelian Tătaru, I believe I understand what happened. I don't think Aurelian was afraid to make love with a young and beautiful woman, even if she *had* been a patient of his. He became frightened and turned white as chalk as soon as he set eyes on her. I believe in that moment he understood the tragedy of Euphrosyne: a half year on earth, and the other half in hell."

"Like Persephone," Albini interrupted, smiling.

"But Euphrosyne wasn't a goddess . . . Before a word was said, Aurelian understood: he had before him a young bacchante, naked and beautiful, and yet he knew that for five or six months a year this bacchante was a woman of seventy. He understood that hell is, in actuality, her existence. And although he was not responsible, because he wasn't the one who decided to suspend the treatment, nevertheless he knew that the tragedy of Euphrosyne was his doing . . . I almost believe that if the accident hadn't occurred, Aurelian Tătaru would have put an end to his life anyway."

"You exaggerate," interrupted Albini. "Dr. Tătaru was a man of science. He knew, or rather he believed, he hoped, that the serum he had discovered would give the expected results. But he hadn't seen the result of the treatment. Perhaps he couldn't believe his eyes . . ." He paused. "At any rate, why are we wasting time on unverifiable hypotheses? We ought, first of all, to congratulate ourselves for all we've found out today. It's a great success! And we owe it all to you."

"To me?"

"Obviously, to you. For motives we don't understand, Comrade Euphrosyne chose you as her confidant instead of Engineer Hagi Pavel. We have today at our disposition the only example—because I no longer dare to say 'person'—the only example which can possibly bring us information about Tătaru's discovery. I mean that the analyses to which Euphrosyne will be subjected will yield clues of the highest values to us. But of course that is not *our* business . . . Probably you've been making corrections at the laboratory. I don't see them on the table . . ."

"At the laboratory," Zalomit repeated absently. "Where I could verify the sketches and the bibliography."

"Three massive volumes all at once!" Albini interrupted. "Three massive volumes. I'm impressed!"

Zalomit felt his cheeks burning again, and he tried to smile.

"As I wrote to you last fall, I'm grateful to you," he managed to say after swallowing several times.

"I have but a single merit: I called the matter to the attention of the right people. Although, I confess, all you communicated to us about Goethe's *Morphology of Plants* . . ."

Zalomit burst out laughing with a slight air of triumph. "This I knew from the start!"

"But it was not known what would follow," continued Albini. "And to us what followed was of the *greatest* interest. By the way," he added, smiling, "it wasn't your fault you didn't succeed in finding Father Calinic last summer. Looking for him among the sheepfolds was futile. He died, poor fellow, that very night after you had separated. Died of exhaustion or old age along the side of the road."

"Information and Investigation," whispered Zalomit after a moment, smiling wanly. And then he added in a voice perhaps intended to be provocative, "He was a saint!"

"Very true. He was a saint. Because he never told anyone how he was tortured, nor why he was tortured. The same lack of imagination of which we spoke last summer, at Poiana Dornei. They imagined they'd find it out from him . . . But, after all, it's futile to evoke the errors of the past. In any event, one thing is certain: Dr. Tătaru did not pass on to anyone—neither friends nor colleagues, nor even to Father Calinic—the secret of the formula. What seems truly curious is the fact that even in his papers no clue of any sort has been found. And yet it's known that his preliminary experiments at the laboratory of the Faculty of Medicine lasted several years. Probably he burned all his notes."

"Probably he burned them," Zalomit echoed mechanically.

"Therefore, as I said, we have nothing but Euphrosyne. It is nevertheless something. Especially since we have also you."

"Me?" asked Zalomit, frightened. "Me?"

Albini began to laugh, taking out a package of cigarettes and a lighter, without haste. "Even you, Professor Doctor Filip Zalomit, author of three massive volumes about Carpathian flora."

"Ah, yes! I understand," said Zalomit, blushing once more.

"Actually, it's a matter of an easy mission, and even, in a certain sense, a pleasant one. You can observe, from time to time—how to say it?—the metamorphosis of one of the Three Graces."

Zalomit swallowed several times, trying in vain to recover his voice.

"I repeat, from time to time. For instance, in March, and again in the *wunderschöne Monat Mai,* and then, at the approach of the summer solstice."

"But why I?" Zalomit succeeded in whispering. "I'm not trained in medical biology."

"Because Euphrosyne knows and trusts you. If we intervene harshly, we'll frighten her. She'll be afraid we hold her responsible for Dr. Tătaru's accident. But you can explain what the situation is and it won't be hard for you to convince her that it's in her interest and the interest of science—especially in the interest of Romanian science—to remain from here on at the disposition of investigators."

"It will be hard," Zalomit began, suddenly recovering his voice. "I don't know if I can take such a responsibility."

"We'll talk about it later," Albini said cheerfully. "You needn't decide now."

He became silent for a time, smoking and looking at him with a curiosity he did not try to hide. "I don't believe I'm being too indiscreet to ask you this: was *Dna* Sidonia Vâlceanu at one time your wife?"

Without intending to, and without knowing why, Zalomit burst out laughing. "It's no indiscretion. We were married when we were both young. I hadn't yet passed my doctorate. And we separated very soon, before the end of the year . . . But we've remained friends."

"This I found out," said Albini, meticulously extinguishing the cigarette. "I know you're still friends. Moreover, we'll be meeting in a few days at the nuptials of Isidora."

"On December 22," said Zalomit, smiling dreamily. "In three days."

"The lucky groom is a cousin of mine. A cousin and a very good friend as well, although he's much younger than I. But I don't wish to detain you," he added, rising from the armchair. "I'm glad, however, that in a certain sense we'll belong to the same family."

"A family of investigators," observed Zalomit, a broad smile lighting his face.

"Very true. Emil Butnaru, my cousin and friend, is an eminent chemist."

Approaching the door, he turned his head abruptly and asked, "Any poetry?"

Zalomit put his hand familiarly on the other man's shoulder and broke into laughter. "Wasn't *Stained Corollas* enough? And do you know any title more prophetic than *Stained Corollas*?"

Albini extended his hand, smiling. "I won't wish you happy holidays, because we'll be meeting in three days at the wedding."

After he closed the door, Zalomit burst into laughter again. This time he laughed without restraint, now and then wiping tears from his cheeks, without knowing what was the matter with him or whence had arisen this joy like nothing he had felt since youth. "It's as though all the world is mine!" he exclaimed, remembering Euphrosyne's words. "How true is it! Because, indeed, the whole world is mine!"

He sat down at the desk, stilling with difficulty the last twitches of laughter and wiping away the tears. "Aurelian," he said aloud as if the doctor were present, "Aurelian, I understand you very well. You were right, there was no other solution."

Suddenly he rose, took the full ashtray, and started for the kitchen. But he changed his mind, went to the window instead and opened it. When he turned around, he was enveloped in cold, clean air, smelling of snow. They knew about Calinic too, he remembered, trying to close the window. They knew about Calinic too. But I don't understand why he removed the microphone in my presence. Perhaps to show me they have all the rights and they do what they want. In a certain sense he was right. Once I agreed to work for them . . . We're becoming part of the same family now . . . And the excuses I made to myself, that I had to accept all this in order to recover the lost formula for the treatment . . .

Suddenly he remembered about the old woman, and he shuddered. Seating himself at his desk, he realized he was shaking. I left the window open too long and I caught a chill. But how could Albini imagine that I could ever bear to meet with her? Fortunately, I'm past sixty, and, above all, fortunately there's the vial. He smiled melancholically, remembering the ritual by which, on that summer afternoon, he had removed the vial from the briefcase and lifting it with a melodramatic gesture in order to gaze upon it at a distance he had recited from Faust's soliloquy: *Ich grüsse dich, du einzige Phiole.* Nothing had happened yet then—neither Aurelian Tătaru's accident nor the encounters with Albini, Father Calinic, and Euphrosyne—and yet as a precaution he had prepared in secret the most concentrated solution of aconite he could obtain in his laboratory.

He was trembling more and more, as though wracked by chills. Opening the drawer with difficulty, he began to search underneath the large manila envelopes in which he kept important letters. After a while, he was seized with a sudden uneasiness, and he rose to his feet and began to pull out the envelopes one by one, tossing them at random on the desk. He stared wild-eyed at the bottom of the drawer. "They looked here too," he whispered. "And they found it!" Feeling his legs giving way beneath him, he sat down, breathing hard. "There's nothing to be done now," he whispered. "I believe there's nothing to be done." He repeated the words with difficulty, as though he were exhausted by an incomprehensible weariness.

Coming to his senses later, he sprang frightened to his feet. He looked anxiously about him, trying to comprehend where he was. *Euphorbia moldavica id est impudica.* He tried to find rhymes: *moldavica . . . impudica.* But he could not concentrate; the barking of the dog exasperated him. A large black dog was circling around him at a distance of a few meters on the gravel. "Here, doggie!" he called in jest, trying to calm him. Then his eyes fell on a bronze plaque, and he read: *Les Trois Grâces*. Of course! Now I understand! he whispered happily. They are three and yet one; the same body, although they're separate. A perfect, serene beauty. No other name would suit them.

WITH THE GYPSY GIRLS

INSIDE the streetcar the heat was scorching, stifling. Walking quickly down the aisle, he said to himself, "You're in luck, Gavrilescu!" He had spotted an empty seat beside an open window at the other end of the car. Once seated, he took out his handkerchief and for a long time sat there mopping his brow and his cheeks. Then he stuffed the handkerchief under his collar all the way around his neck and began fanning himself with his straw hat. An old man sitting across from him had been staring at him the whole time, as if trying to recall where he had seen him before. He was holding a metal box very carefully on his knees.

"This heat is awful!" he said all of a sudden. "It hasn't been this hot since 1905!"

Gavrilescu nodded and continued to fan himself with his hat. "It certainly is hot," he said. "But when a man is cultured, he can stand anything more easily. Colonel Lawrence, for instance. Do you know anything about Colonel Lawrence?"

"No."

"Too bad—I don't know much about him either. If those young men had got on this streetcar, I would have asked them. I always like to strike up a conversation with cultured people. Those young men, sir, must have been students. Outstanding students. We were all waiting together at the car stop, and I listened to what they were saying. They were talking about a certain Colonel Lawrence and his adventures in Arabia. And what memories they had! They were reciting by heart whole pages from the colonel's book.* There was one sentence I particularly liked, a very beautiful sentence, about the intense heat he encountered—the colonel, that is—somewhere in Arabia, which smote him on the top of the head, smote him like a saber. Too bad I can't remember it word for word. That terrible heat of Arabia smote him like a saber. It smote him on the top of the head like a saber, and struck him dumb."

The conductor, who had been listening with a smile, handed him his ticket. Gavrilescu put his hat on his head and began searching through his pockets.

"Excuse me," he murmured finally, when he was unable to find his wallet. "I never know where I put it."

"That's all right," said the conductor, with unexpected good humor. "We've got time—we haven't got to the gypsy girls' yet."

And turning to the old man, he winked at him. The old man blushed and nervously held on to the metal box more tightly, with both hands. Gavrilescu handed the conductor a bill, and he began counting out the change, still smiling.

"It's a scandal!" muttered the old man after a few moments. "It's a crime!"

"Everybody's talking about them," said Gavrilescu, starting to fan himself again with his hat. "It certainly is a fine-looking house, and what a garden! What a garden!" he repeated, nodding his head in admiration. "Look, you can almost see it from here," he added, leaning forward a little in order to see better.

A number of men moved their heads closer to the windows, as if by chance.

---

*Mircea Eliade himself as a young man translated T. E. Lawrence's *Revolt in the Desert* into Romanian, under the title *Revolta în Deşert* (Bucharest 1934).—TRANSLATOR'S NOTE.

"It's a scandal!" the old man repeated, looking severely straight in front of him. "It ought to be forbidden."

"They have some ancient walnut trees," continued Gavrilescu. "That's why it's so shady and cool there. I've heard that walnut trees begin to throw a thick shade only after thirty or forty years. Do you suppose that's true?"

But the old man pretended not to hear. Gavrilescu turned to one of his neighbors, who had been gazing out of the window lost in thought.

"They have some ancient walnut trees which must be at least fifty years old," he began. "That's why there's so much shade. And in the heat like this, that's a real pleasure. Those lucky people!"

"Lucky girls," said his neighbor, without raising his eyes. "They're gypsy girls."

"That's what I've heard too," continued Gavrilescu. "I ride on this streetcar three times a week. And I give you my word of honor, never once has it happened that I didn't hear people talking about them, about the gypsy girls. Does anyone know who they are? I wonder where they came from?"

"They came here a long time ago," said his neighbor.

"They've been here twenty-one years," someone interrupted him. "When I first came to Bucureşti, the gypsy girls were already here. But the garden was much larger. The lyceum hadn't been built yet."

"As I was telling you," Gavrilescu began again, "I ride this streetcar regularly three times a week. Unfortunately for me, I'm a piano teacher. I say unfortunately for me," he added, with an attempt at a smile, "because that's not what I was made for. I have the soul of an artist."

"Why then I know you," said the old man suddenly, turning his head. "You're *Domnul* Gavrilescu, the piano teacher. I have a little granddaughter, and you've been giving her lessons for five or six years now. I've been wondering the whole time why your face was so familiar."

"Yes, that's me," Gavrilescu resumed. "I give piano lessons and I travel a lot by streetcar. In the spring, when it's not too hot and there's a breeze blowing, it's a real pleasure. You sit at a window like this, and as the streetcar goes along you see lots of gardens in bloom. As I was telling you, I travel on this line three times a week. And I always hear people talking about the gypsy girls. Many times I've asked myself, 'Gavrilescu,' I say to myself, 'assuming they're gypsies, I wonder where they get so much money?' A house like that, a real palace, with gardens and ancient walnut trees—that takes millions."

"It's a scandal!" the old man exclaimed again, turning his head away in disgust.

"And I've also asked myself another question," continued Gavrilescu. "In terms of what I earn, a hundred lei a lesson, it would take ten thousand lessons to make a million. But you see, things aren't as simple as that. Let's say I had twenty lessons a week, it would still take me five hundred weeks—in other words almost ten years—and I would have to have twenty pupils with twenty pianos. And then there's the problem of summer vacations, when I'm left with only two or three pupils. And Christmas and Easter vacations too. All those lost lessons are lost for the million too—so that I shouldn't speak of five hundred weeks with twenty lessons, and twenty pupils with twenty pianos, but of much more than that, much more!"

"That's right," said one of his neighbors. "These days people don't learn to play the piano anymore."

"Oh!" exclaimed Gavrilescu suddenly, tapping his forehead with his hat. "I thought I'd forgotten something, but I couldn't think what it was. My portfolio! I forgot the portfolio with my music. I stopped to chat with Mrs. Voitinovici, Otilia's aunt, and I forget the portfolio. Of all the luck!" he added, pulling the handkerchief out from under his collar and stuffing it in his pocket. "In all this heat, back you go, Gavrilescu, all the way back on the streetcar to Strada Preoteselor."*

---

*"Street of the Priests' Wives."—TRANSLATOR'S NOTE.

He looked about him desperately, as if he expected someone to stop him. Then he stood up suddenly.

"It's been a pleasure meeting you," he said, lifting his hat and bowing slightly from the waist.

Then he quickly stepped out onto the platform just as the car was stopping. Alighting on the street, he was again enveloped in the intense heat and the smell of melted asphalt. With some difficulty he crossed the street to wait for the streetcar going in the opposite direction. "Gavrilescu," he murmured, "watch out! for it looks . . . it really looks as if you're starting to grow old. You're getting decrepit, you're losing your memory. Again I say, watch out! because there's no excuse for it. At forty-nine a man is in the prime of life."

But he felt worn out and weary, and he sank down on the bench, right out in the sun. He pulled out his handkerchief and began to mop his face. "Somehow this reminds me of something," he said to himself to give himself courage. "A little effort, Gavrilescu, a little effort of the memory. Somewhere, on a bench, without a cent in my pocket. It wasn't as hot as this, but it was summer just the same." He looked around him at the deserted street, at the houses with the shutters drawn and the blinds lowered as if they had been abandoned. "Everybody is going to the shore," he said to himself, "and tomorrow or the day after Otilia is going too." And then it came to him: it was in Charlottenburg; he was sitting, just as he was now, on a bench in the sun, only then he was hungry and hadn't a cent in his pocket. "When you're young and an artist, you can bear anything more easily," he said to himself. He stood up and took a few steps out into the street to see if the streetcar was in sight. As he walked, it seemed as if the heat was losing some of its intensity. He returned, and leaning against the wall of a house, took off his hat and began fanning himself.

A hundred meters or so up the street was what looked like an oasis of shade. From inside a garden the branches of a tall linden tree with their dense foliage hung down over the sidewalk. Gavrilescu looked at them, fascinated but hesitating. He turned his head once more to see if the streetcar was coming, then set off determinedly, taking long steps and keeping close to the walls. When he got there, the shade did not seem so thick. But the coolness of the garden could still be felt, and Gavrilescu began to breathe deeply, throwing his head back a little. "What must it have been like a month ago, with the lindens all in flower!" he said to himself dreamily. He went up to the iron grillwork gate and gazed in at the garden. The gravel had recently been wet down, and one could see beds of flowers, while farther back was a pool with statues of dwarves around the edge. At that moment he heard the streetcar pass by him with a dry screech, and he turned his head. "Too late!" he exclaimed with a smile. "*Zu spät!*" he added, and raising his arm, he waved farewell several times with his hat, as at the North Station in the good old days, when Elsa was leaving to spend a month with her family in a village near Munich.

Then, sensibly and without haste, he continued on his way. On reaching the next stop he took off his coat and prepared to wait, when all at once he caught the rather bitter odor of walnut leaves crushed between the fingers. He turned his head and looked around him. He was alone. As far as eye could see, the sidewalk was empty. He didn't dare look up at the sky, but he felt above his head that same dazzling, incandescent, white light, and he felt the scorching heat of the street strike him on the mouth and cheeks. Then he set off again resignedly, his coat under his arm and his hat pulled down firmly on his forehead. Seeing from a distance the heavy shade of the walnut trees, he felt his heart beat faster, and he quickened his pace a little. He had almost reached there when he heard the metallic screech of the streetcar behind him. He stopped and waved his hat after it for a long time. "Too late!" he exclaimed. "Too late!"

. . .

In the shade of the walnut tree he was bathed in an unexpected, unnatural coolness, and Gavrilescu stood there a moment, bewildered but smiling. It was as if he suddenly found himself in a forest up in the mountains. In astonishment he began to look almost with awe at the tall trees and the stone wall covered with ivy, and gradually an infinite sadness stole over him. For so many years he had been going past this garden on the streetcar, without even once having the curiosity to get off and take a closer look at it. He walked along slowly, his head thrown back a little, his gaze fixed on the tall tops of the trees. And all at once he found himself just outside the gate, and there, as if she had been hiding a long time watching him, a young girl stepped out in front of him, beautiful and very swarthy, with a golden necklace and big golden earrings. Taking him by the arm, she asked him in a soft voice:

"Are you looking for the gypsy girls?"

She smiled at him with her whole mouth and with her eyes; and seeing him hesitate, she pulled him gently by the arm into the yard. Gavrilescu followed her, fascinated; but after a few steps he stopped, as if he wanted to say something.

"Won't you come to the gypsy girls'?" the girl asked him again, in a still softer voice.

She looked him in the eye fleetingly but deeply, then took his hand and quickly led him to a little old house, which you would scarcely have guessed was there, hidden among lilac and dwarf elder bushes. She opened the door and gently pushed him inside. Gavrilescu found himself in a curious semidarkness, as if the windows had blue and green panes. Far away he heard the streetcar approaching, and the metallic screech struck him as so unbearable that he put his hand to his forehead. When the racket died away he discovered near him, seated at a short-legged table, with a cup of coffee in front of her, an old woman who was looking at him curiously, as if waiting for him to wake up.

"What is your heart's desire for today?" she asked him. "A gypsy girl, a Greek girl, a German girl?"

"No," Gavrilescu interrrupted her, raising his arm, "not a German girl."

"Well then, a gypsy girl, a Greek girl, a Jewish girl?" the old woman went on. "Three hundred lei," she added.

Gavrilescu smiled, but it was a grave smile.

"Three piano lessons!" he exclaimed, beginning to search his pockets. "And that's not counting the round trip on the streetcar."

The old woman took a sip of coffee and seemed lost in thought.

"You're a musician?" she asked him suddenly. "Then I'm sure you'll be satisfied."

"I am an artist," said Gavrilescu, taking a number of wet handkerchiefs out of one trousers pocket, one after the other, and transferring them methodically, one by one, to the other. "Unfortunately for me, I became a piano teacher, but my ideal has always been art for its own sake. I live for the soul. I'm sorry," he added, a bit embarrassed, setting his hat on the little table and putting in it the things he was taking out of his pockets. "I never can find my wallet when I need it."

"There's no hurry," said the old woman. "We've got lots of time. It's not even three o'clock yet."

"I'm sorry to contradict you," Gavrilescu interrupted her, "but I think you're mistaken. It must be almost four. It was three when I finished the lesson with Otilia."

"Then the clock must have stopped again," murmured the old woman, and once again was lost in thought.

"There, at last!" exclaimed Gavrilescu, showing her the wallet triumphantly. "It was right where it was supposed to be."

He counted out the bills and handed them to her.

"Take him to the cottage," said the old woman, raising her eyes.

Gavrilescu felt someone take his hand. Startled, he turned his head and saw beside him once again the girl who had lured him into entering the gate. He followed her timidly, holding under his arm the hat loaded with the things from his pockets.

"Now remember them well," the girl told him, "and don't get them mixed up: a gypsy girl, a Greek girl, a Jewish girl."

They crossed the garden, passing in front of the tall building with the red-tiled roof which Gavrilescu had seen from the street.

She stopped and looked deep into his eyes for a moment, then burst out in a brief, soft laugh. Gavrilescu had just started to put all the things from his hat back in his pockets.

"Oh!" he said. "I am an artist. If I had any choice in the matter, I would stay here, in these groves," and he waved his hat toward the trees. "I love nature. And in all this heat, to be able to breathe pure air, to enjoy a coolness like that in the mountains. But where are we going?" he asked, seeing that the girl was approaching a wooden fence and opening the gate.

"To the cottage. That's what the old woman said."

She took his arm again and led him along after her. They entered a neglected garden, with roses and lilies lost among the weeds and sweetbrier bushes. The heat was beginning to make itself felt again, and Gavrilescu hesitated, disappointed.

"I was deceiving myself," he said. "I came here for coolness, for nature."

"Wait till you go in the cottage," the girl interrupted him, pointing to a little old house, rather ramshackle-looking, which could be seen at the end of the garden.

Gavrilescu put his hat on and followed her morosely. But when he reached the vestibule, he felt his heart beating faster and faster, and he stopped.

"I'm all excited, " he said, "and I don't know why."

"Don't drink too much coffee," the girl said softly, as she opened the door and pushed him inside.

It was a room whose limits he could not see, for the curtains were drawn, and in the semidarkness the screens looked like the walls. He started to walk forward into the room, treading on carpets each one thicker and softer than the last, as if he were stepping on mattresses, and at every step his heart beat faster, until finally he was afraid to go any farther, and he stopped. At that moment he suddenly felt happy, as if he had become young again, and the whole world was his, and Hildegard too was his.

"Hildegard!" he exclaimed, addressing the girl. "I haven't thought of her for twenty years. She was my great love. She was the woman of my life!"

But on turning his head, he found that the girl had left. Then his nostrils caught a subtle, exotic scent, and suddenly he heard hands clapping, while the room began to get light in a mysterious way, as if the curtains were being drawn back slowly, very slowly, one by one, allowing the light of the summer afternoon to come in a little at a time. But Gavrilescu scarcely had time to notice that not one of the curtains had been touched, when he caught sight of three young girls standing a few meters in front of him, clapping their hands softly and laughing.

"We're the ones you chose," said one of them. "A gypsy girl, a Greek girl, a Jewish girl."

"Now let's see if you can guess which is which," said the second.

"Let's see if you know which is the gypsy girl," added the third.

Gavrilescu had dropped his straw hat and was looking at them with a vacant stare, transfixed, as if he didn't see them, as if he were looking at something else, beyond them, beyond the screens.

"I'm thirsty!" he whispered all at once, putting his hand to his throat.

"The old woman sent you some coffee," said one of the girls.

She disappeared behind a screen and returned with a round wooden tray on which were a cup of coffee and a coffeepot. Gavrilescu took the cup and drank it all down, then handed it back to her with a smile.

"I'm terribly thirsty," he murmured.

"This will be very hot, for it's right out of the pot," said the girl, refilling his cup. "Drink it slowly."

Gavrilescu tried to sip it, but the coffee was so hot that he burned his lips, and he put the cup back on the tray, disappointed.

"I'm thirsty!" he said again. "If I could just have a little drink of water!"

The other two girls disappeared behind the screen and returned at once with two full trays.

"The old woman sent you some jam," said one of them.

"Rose jam and sherbert," added the other.

But Gavrilescu saw only the jug full of water, and although he had noticed the heavy, frosted, green-glass tumbler beside it, he seized the jug with both hands and put it to his lips. He took his time, drinking in noisy gulps, with his head thrown back. Then he heaved a sigh, set the jug back on the tray, and took one of the handkerchiefs out of his pocket.

"Ladies!" he exclaimed, starting to mop his brow. "I really was awfully thirsty. I've heard about a man, Colonel Lawrence . . ."

The girls exchanged knowing glances, then all burst out laughing. This time they laughed unrestrainedly, harder and harder as time went on. At first Gavrilescu gazed at them in astonishment, then a broad smile crept over his face, and finally he too began to laugh. He mopped his face for a long time with the handkerchief.

"If I too may ask a question," he said at last, "I'd be curious to know what got into you."

"We were laughing because you called us ladies," said one of them. "Did you forget you're with the gypsy girls?"

"That's not so!" another interrupted. "Don't pay any attention to her, she's just trying to fool you. We were laughing because you got mixed up and drank from the jug instead of the glass. If you had drunk from the glass . . ."

"Don't listen to her!" the third interrupted. "She's just trying to fool you. I'll tell you the real truth: we were laughing because you were afraid."

"That's not so! That's not so!" the other two burst out. "She wanted to test you, to see if you were afraid."

"He was afraid! He was afraid!" repeated the third girl.

Gavrilescu took a step forward and raised his arm solemnly.

"Ladies!" he cried, offended. "I see you don't know who you have before you. I'm not just anybody. I'm Gavrilescu, the artist. And before becoming, unfortunately for me, a miserable piano teacher, I experienced a poet's dream. Ladies," he exclaimed with emotion, after a pause, "when I was twenty I knew, I fell in love with, I adored Hildegard!"

One of the girls brought up an armchair for him, and Gavrilescu sat down with a deep sigh.

"Ah!" he began after a long silence. "Why have you reminded me of the tragedy of my life? Because, you understand, Hildegard never became my wife. Something happened, something terrible happened."

The girl handed him the cup of coffee, and Gavrilescu began to sip it, pensively.

"Something terrible happened," he resumed, after some time. "But what? What could have happened? It's strange that I can't remember. Of course, I hadn't thought of Hildegard for many, many years. I had grown accustomed to the situation. I told myself: 'Gavrilescu, the past is past. That's the way it is with artists—they never have any luck.' And then suddenly, just now, when I came in here to you, I remembered that I too have known a noble passion, I remembered that I have loved Hildegard!"

The girls exchanged glances and began to clap their hands.

"So I was right after all," said the third girl. "He was afraid."

"Yes," the others agreed. "You were right: he was afraid."

Gavrilescu raised his eyes and looked at them sadly for a long time.

"I don't understand what you mean."

"You are afraid," one of the girls proclaimed tauntingly, taking a step toward him. "You've been afraid from the moment you first came in."

"That's why you were so thirsty," said the second.

"And ever since then you keep changing the subject," added the other. "You chose us, but you're afraid to guess which is which."

"I still don't understand," said Gavrilescu defensively.

"You should have guessed right at the start," continued the third girl. "You should have guessed which is the gypsy girl, which is the Greek girl, and which the Jewish girl."

"Try it now, since you say you're not afraid," the first one said again. "Which is the gypsy girl?"

"Which is the gypsy girl? Which is the gypsy girl?" The voices of the others came to Gavrilescu like an echo.

He smiled and looked at them again searchingly.

"How do you like that!" he began, suddenly feeling in high spirits. "Now that you've finally grasped the fact that I'm an artist, you think I live up in the clouds and don't know what a gypsy girl looks like."

"Don't change the subject again," one of the girls interrupted him. "Guess!"

"I mean," Gavrilescu continued stubbornly, "you think I don't have sufficient imagination to pick out the gypsy girl, especially when she's young, beautiful, and naked."

For of course he had guessed which was which as soon as he set eyes on them. The one who had taken a step toward him, completely naked, very swarthy, with black hair and eyes, was without doubt the gypsy girl. The second girl was naked too, but covered with a pale green veil; her body was preternaturally white, so that it gleamed like mother-of-pearl; on her feet she wore gilded slippers. She could only be the Greek girl. The third was without doubt the Jewish girl: she had on a long skirt of cherry-colored velvet, which hugged her body at the waist, leaving her breasts and shoulders bare; her abundant hair, red with fiery glints, was skillfully braided and piled on the top of her head.

"Guess! Which is the gypsy girl? Which is the gypsy girl?" cried all three.

Gavrilescu suddenly got up from the chair, and pointing to the naked, swarthy girl in front of him, he pronounced solemnly: "Since I am an artist, I consent to be put to the test, even such a childish test as this, and I respond: You are the gypsy girl!"

The next instant he felt himself taken by the hands, and the girls began turning him round and round, shouting and whistling; their voices seemed to come to him from very far away.

"You didn't guess it! You didn't guess it!" he heard as if in a dream.

He tried to stop, to escape from those hands which were turning him around at such a furious pace, as if in a witches' dance, but it was beyond his power to tear himself loose. His nostrils were filled with the emanation of their young bodies and that exotic, remote perfume, and he heard inside himself, but also outside of himself, on the carpet, the sound of the girls' feet dancing. He felt at the same time how the dance was carrying him gently between chairs and screens toward the other end of the room. After a time he ceased to resist—and was no longer aware of anything.

. . .

When he awoke, he found the swarthy, naked girl kneeling on the carpet in front of the sofa, and he sat up.

"Did I sleep very long?" he asked her.

"You weren't really asleep," the girl reassured him. "You just dozed a little."

"But what on earth have you done to me?" he asked, putting his hand to his forehead. "I feel as if I'd been drugged."

He looked around him in amazement. It no longer looked

like the same room, and yet, scattered among the armchairs, sofas, and mirrors were the screens which had made such an impression on him from the moment he entered. He couldn't see any rhyme or reason to the way they were arranged. Some were very tall, almost touching the ceiling, and might have been mistaken for walls, except that here and there they projected at acute angles out into the middle of the room. Others, lighted up in some mysterious way, looked like windows, half covered with curtains, opening on interior corridors. And other screens, many-colored and curiously painted, or covered with shawls and embroideries, which fell in folds to the carpets and merged with them, were placed in such a way, you would have said, as to form alcoves of various shapes and sizes. But he had only to fix his gaze for a moment or two on one such alcove in order to realize that it was all an illusion, that what he was really seeing was two or three separate screens whose reflections in a large mirror with a greenish-gold shimmer caused them to appear to be joined together. At the very moment that he became aware of the illusion, Gavrilescu felt the room start turning around him, and he put his hand to his forehead again.

"What on earth have you done to me?" he repeated.

"You didn't guess who I am," the girl said softly, with a sad smile. "And yet I winked at you as a sign that *I'm* not the gypsy girl. I'm the Greek girl."

"Greece!" exclaimed Gavrilescu, getting to his feet suddenly. "Eternal Greece!"

His weariness seemed to have vanished as if by magic. He could hear his heart beating faster, and a bliss never before experienced suffused his entire body with a warm throb.

"When I was in love with Hildegard," he continued enthusiastically, "that's all we dreamed of—taking a trip to Greece together."

"You were a fool," the girl interrupted him. "You shouldn't have been dreaming, you should have loved her."

"I was twenty and she wasn't quite eighteen. She was beautiful. We were both beautiful," he added.

At that moment he became aware that he was dressed in a strange costume: he had on wide pantaloons, like Indian shalwars, and a short tunic of golden-yellow silk. He looked at himself in the mirror with astonishment, and had some difficulty even recognizing himself.

"We dreamed of going to Greece," he continued after a few moments, in a calmer voice. "No, it was much more than a dream, for we had plans to make it come true: we had decided to leave for Greece right after the wedding. And then something happened. But what on earth could have happened?" he asked himself after a pause, putting both hands to his temples. "Everything was just the same, a day as hot as this, a terrible summer day. I saw a bench and started toward it, and then I felt the intense heat smite me on the top of the head, smite me like a saber on the top of the head. No, that's what happened to Colonel Lawrence; I heard about it today from some students while I was waiting for the streetcar. Oh, if I only had a piano!" he exclaimed in despair.

The girl sprang to her feet, and taking his hand, said softly, "Come with me!"

She led him quickly between the screens and mirrors, going faster and faster, and before long Gavrilescu found himself running. He wanted to stop a moment to catch his breath, but the girl wouldn't let him.

"It's late!" she murmured as she ran; and again her voice seemed to him like the sound of a whistle reaching him from far away.

But this time he didn't get dizzy, although as they ran he had to avoid innumerable soft sofas and cushions, chests and boxes covered with rugs, and mirrors large and small, some of them cut in strange shapes, which unexpectedly appeared in front of them, as though they had just been put there. All of a sudden they emerged from a sort of corridor formed by two rows of screens and entered a large, sunny room. There, leaning against a piano, the other two girls were waiting for them.

"Why are you so late?" the red-haired one asked them. "The coffee's gotten cold."

Gavrilescu caught his breath, and taking a step toward her, raised both arms as if to defend himself.

"Oh, no," he said, "I won't drink any more. I've drunk enough coffee. Though I have the soul of an artist, ladies, I lead a regular life. I don't like to waste my time in cafés."

But as if she hadn't heard him, the girl turned to the Greek girl.

"Why are you so late?" she asked again.

"He thought of Hildegard."

"You shouldn't have let him," said the third girl.

"Pardon, allow me," Gavrilescu broke in, approaching the piano. "This is a strictly personal matter. No one else has any right to interfere. It was the tragedy of my life."

"Now he'll be late again," said the red-haired girl. "He's confused all over again."

"Allow me," Gavrilescu burst out. "I'm not at all confused. It was the tragedy of my life. I thought of her when I first entered here. Listen!" he exclaimed, approaching the piano again. "I'll play you something and then you'll understand."

"You shouldn't have let him," he heard the two girls whisper. "Now he'll never guess us."

Gavrilescu sat there a few moments concentrating, then hunched his shoulders over the keyboard as if he were about to attack *con brio*.

"Now I remember!" he exclaimed all at once. "I know what happened!"

He got up from the piano bench in excitement and began pacing the floor, his gaze fixed on the carpet.

"Now I know," he repeated several times, in a low voice. "It was just like now, it was in the summer. Hildegard had left with her family for Königsberg. It was terribly hot. I was living in Charlottenburg, and had gone out for a walk under the trees. They were tall, ancient trees, with heavy shade. Everything was deserted. It was too hot. No one dared leave the house. And there under the trees I came upon a young girl sobbing bitterly, sobbing with her face buried in her hands. And there was one surprising thing: she had taken off her shoes and was resting her feet on a small suitcase lying on the pavement in front of her. 'Gavrilescu,' I said to myself, 'there's an unhappy creature.' How could I guess that . . ."

Suddenly he stopped and turned abruptly to the girls.

"Ladies!" he exclaimed with emotion. "I was young, I was handsome, and I had the soul of an artist. An abandoned girl simply rent my heart. I stopped to talk with her and tried to console her. And that's how the tragedy of my life began."

"And now what are we to do?" asked the red-haired girl, addressing the others.

"Let's wait and see what the old chatterbox says," said the Greek girl.

"If we wait any longer, he'll never guess us," said the third girl.

"Yes, the tragedy of my life," continued Gavrilescu. "Her name was Elsa . . . But I became resigned to it. I said to myself, 'Gavrilescu, thus it was written. An evil hour!' That's the way artists are, they never have any luck."

"See!" said the red-haired girl. "He's getting all confused again, and he'll never be able to straighten himself out."

"Ah, fate!" exclaimed Gavrilescu, raising both arms in the air and turning toward the Greek girl.

The girl looked at him with a smile, her hands joined behind her back.

"Eternal Greece!" he continued. "I never did get to see you."

"Stop that! Stop that!" cried the other two girls, coming closer to him. "Remember how you chose us!"

"A gypsy girl, a Greek girl, a Jewish girl," said the Greek

girl, looking him deeply and significantly in the eye. "That's the way you wanted it, that's the way you chose us."

"Guess us," cried the red-haired girl, "and you'll see how nice everything will be."

"Which is the gypsy girl? Which is the gypsy girl?" asked all three at once, surrounding him.

Gavrilescu retreated quickly and leaned against the piano.

"Well," he began after a pause, "that may be the way *you* think things are here. Artist or ordinary mortal, you've got a good thing going: I have to guess the gypsy girl. But why, I ask you? Who gave the order?"

"That's our game here at the gypsy girls'," said the Greek girl. "Try and guess. You won't find it so bad."

"But I'm not in the mood to play games," Gavrilescu continued with fervor. "I have remembered the tragedy of my life. And now, you see, I understand very well how it all happened: if on that evening, in Charlottenburg, I had not gone to a beer hall with Elsa . . . Or even if I had gone, but if I had had any money with me, and had been able to pay the check, my life would have been different. But as it happened I had no money, and it was Elsa who paid. And the next day I went all over everywhere looking for a few marks to pay my debt. But I couldn't get any anywhere. All my friends and acquaintances had gone on vacation. It was summer and it was terribly hot."

"He's afraid again," murmured the red-haired girl, with downcast eyes.

"Listen, I haven't told you the whole story," cried Gavrilescu with emotion. "For three days I couldn't find any money, and every evening I would go to see her, Elsa, at her lodgings, to apologize because I hadn't got the money. And afterward we would both go to the beer hall. If only I had been firm and hadn't agreed to go to the beer hall with her! But I couldn't help it, I was hungry. I was young, I was handsome, Hildegard had gone to the shore, and I was hungry. I tell you frankly, there were days when I went to bed with an empty stomach. That's an artist's life for you!"

"And now what are we to do?" the girls asked him. "For time is passing, time is passing."

"Now?" exclaimed Gavrilescu, raising his arms again. "Now it's good and hot, and I like you because you are young and beautiful, and are standing here before me ready to serve me sweets and coffee. But I'm not thirsty anymore. Right now I feel fine, I feel just great. And I say to myself: 'Gavrilescu, these girls expect something of you. Why not oblige them? If they want you to guess them, then guess them. But watch out! Watch out, Gavrilescu, for if you guess wrong again, they'll take you on their wild dance and you won't wake up until dawn.'"

Smiling, he walked around the piano in such a way as to keep it as a shield between himself and the girls.

"So, then, you want me to tell you which one is the gypsy girl. All right then, I'll tell you."

The girls lined up excitedly, without a word, looking him in the eye.

"I'll tell you," he said again, after a pause.

Then he abruptly, melodramatically, raised his arm and pointed at the girl in the pale-green veil, and waited. The girls froze in place, as if they couldn't bring themselves to believe it.

"What's the matter with him?" the red-haired one finally asked. "Why can't he guess us?"

"Something's happened to him," said the Greek girl. "He remembered something, and he's lost his way, he's lost in the past."

The girl he had taken for the gypsy girl came forward a few steps, picked up the coffee tray, and passing in front of the piano, murmured with a sad smile: "I'm the Jewish girl."

Then she disappeared behind a screen without another word.

"Oh!" exclaimed Gavrilescu, striking his forehead. "I should have understood. There was something in her eyes that came from very far away. And she had a veil, which didn't really hide anything, but it was still a veil. It was just like the Old Testament."

Suddenly the red-haired girl burst out laughing.

"The gentleman didn't guess us!" she cried. "He didn't guess which is the gypsy girl."

She ran her hand through her hair. Then, as she shook herself several times, her braids fell, red and fiery, on her shoulders. She began to dance, turning slowly round and round in a circle, clapping her hands and singing.

"Tell him, Greek girl, what it would have been like!" she cried, shaking her braids.

"If you had guessed her, everything would have been wonderful," said the Greek girl softly. "We would have sung for you and danced for you and we would have taken you through all the rooms. It would have been wonderful."

"It would have been wonderful," repeated Gavrilescu with a sad smile.

"Tell him, Greek girl!" cried the gypsy girl, stopping in front of them, but continuing to clap her hands rhythmically and stamping her bare foot harder and harder on the carpet.

The Greek girl moved close to him and began talking. She spoke quickly, in a whisper, occasionally nodding her head or brushing her fingers over her lips. But Gavrilescu couldn't make out what she was saying. He listened to her with a smile, with a faraway look in his eyes, and from time to time he murmured, "It would have been wonderful."

He heard the foot of the gypsy girl stamping on the carpet harder and harder, with a muffled, subterranean sound, until that wild, unfamiliar rhythm became more than he could stand. Then, with a great effort, he dashed to the piano and began to play.

"Now you tell him too, gypsy girl!" cried the Greek girl.

He heard her approach him, as if she were dancing on a huge bronze drum; and a moment later he felt her ardent breath on the back of his neck. Gavrilescu bent still lower over the piano and struck the keyboard with all his force, almost with fury, as if he wanted to send the keys flying, to tear them out, and so make a way for himself with his fingernails right into the belly of the piano, and then farther still, deeper still.

. . .

He was no longer thinking of anything, absorbed as he was in the new, strange melodies, which he seemed to be hearing for the first time; and yet they came to his mind one after the other, as though he were remembering them after a very long time. Finally he stopped, and only then did he realize that he was alone in the room and that it had become almost completely dark.

"Where are you?" he cried in alarm, getting up from the bench.

He hesitated a few moments, then walked over to the screen behind which the Jewish girl had disappeared.

"Where are you hiding?" he called again.

Slowly, walking on tiptoe, as if he wanted to take them by surprise, he slipped behind the screen. Here you would have said a new room began, which seemed to be continued in a winding corridor. It was a curiously constructed room, with a low and irregular ceiling and somewhat serpentine walls that disappeared and reappeared in the darkness. Gavrilescu took a few tentative steps, then stopped to listen. At that very moment he thought he heard rustling sounds and rapid steps on the carpet passing very close to him.

"Where are you?" he called.

He listened to the echo of his voice while trying to penetrate the darkness with his gaze. He thought he caught sight of the three of them hiding in a corner of the corridor, and he headed in that direction, groping with his arms extended in front of him. But he soon realized that he had started off in the wrong direction, for he discovered that after a few meters the corridor turned left and continued a long way in that direction, so he stopped again.

"It's no use hiding, I'll find you just the same!" he called. "Better show yourselves of your own accord!"

He strained to hear, gazing down the corridor. Not a sound could be heard. But then he began to feel the heat again, and he decided to go back and play the piano while waiting for them. The direction from which he had come was fixed in his mind, and he knew he had gone only twenty or thirty steps. He extended his arms and proceeded slowly and cautiously. But after a few steps his hands touched a screen, and he drew back frightened. He was certain the screen had not been there a few moments before.

"What's gotten into you?" he cried. "Let me pass!"

Again he thought he heard stifled laughter and rustling sounds. He plucked up his courage.

"Perhaps you think I'm afraid," he began after a short pause, doing his best to appear in good humor. "Allow me, allow me!" he added quickly, as if he expected to be interrupted. "If I agreed to play hide-and-seek with you, I did so because I was sorry for you. That's the honest truth, I was sorry for you. Right from the start I saw you, innocent girls shut up here in a cottage at the gypsy girls', and I said to myself: 'Gavrilescu, these girls want to play tricks on you. Pretend to be taken in. Let them think you can't guess which is the gypsy girl. It's all part of the game!' It's all part of the game!" he shouted as loud as he could. "But now we've been playing long enough; come on out into the light!"

He stopped to listen, smiling, his right hand resting on the screen. At that moment he heard the sound of quick steps in the darkness, very close to him. He turned suddenly and extended his arms in front of him.

"Let's see which one of you it is," he said. "Let's see whom I've caught. Did I catch the gypsy girl?"

But after waving his arms around for some time, hardly realizing what he was doing, he stopped again to listen, and this time not the slightest sound reached him from any direction.

"It doesn't matter," he said, as if he knew that the girls

were there somewhere nearby, hiding in the darkness. "We can wait. I see you still don't know whom you have to deal with. Later on you'll be sorry. I could have taught you to play the piano. Your musical culture would have been enriched. I would have explained Schumann's *Lieder* to you. What beauty!" he exclaimed with fervor. "What divine music!"

Now he could feel the heat again, and it seemed hotter than ever. He began to mop his face with the sleeve of his tunic. Then, discouraged, he started off to the left, feeling his way along the screen the whole time. From time to time he stopped to listen, then continued again at a faster pace.

"Why did I ever allow myself to be pitted against a bunch of girls?" he burst out all at once, suddenly overcome with anger. "Pardon me! I said girls out of courtesy. But you're something else. You know very well what you are. You're gypsies. Completely lacking in culture. Illiterate. Does any one of you know where Arabia is? Has any one of you ever heard of Colonel Lawrence?"

The screen seemed to be endless, and the farther he went, the more unbearable the heat became. He took off his tunic, and after furiously mopping his face and neck, he put it over his bare shoulder like a towel, then began groping with both arms extended once more, trying to find the screen again. But this time he encountered a smooth, cool wall, and he clung to it with outstretched arms. He remained thus a long time, clinging to the wall and breathing deeply. Then he began to move slowly, keeping close to the wall and inching his way along it. After a time he discovered that he had lost his tunic, and as he was still perspiring constantly he stopped, took off his shalwars, and began mopping his face and his whole body. Just then he thought he felt something touch his shoulder, and with a shriek he jumped aside, frightened.

"Let me pass!" he cried. "I told you to let me pass!"

Again someone or something, a creature or an object whose nature he could not determine, touched him on the face and shoulders; at that he began whirling his shalwars blindly over his head in an effort to defend himself. He felt hotter and hotter, he could feel the drops of sweat trickling down his cheeks, and he was gasping for breath. Suddenly, as he swung them around too vigorously, the shalwars flew out of his hand and disappeared somewhere far off in the darkness. For a moment Gavrilescu stood there with his arm extended above his head, clenching his fist spasmodically, as if hoping to discover, from one moment to the next, that he had been mistaken, that the shalwars were still in his possession.

All at once it came to him that he was naked, and he made himself as small as possible, dropping to a crouching position, supporting himself with his hands on the carpet, his head lowered, as if he were ready to take to flight. He began to move forward, groping all around him on the carpet with his hands, still hoping he might find the shalwars again. From time to time he encountered things that it was difficult for him to identify. Some at first resembled small chests, but when he felt of them more carefully they turned out to be giant pumpkins draped with kerchiefs. Others, which at first seemed like cushions or bolsters for a sofa, became, upon closer examination, balls, old umbrellas stuffed with bran, laundry baskets full of newspapers—but he didn't really have time to decide what they might be, for he was continually coming across new objects ahead of him, and would start feeling of them. Sometimes big pieces of furniture suddenly loomed up before him, and Gavrilescu cautiously went around them, for he couldn't discern their shapes and was fearful of knocking them over.

He had no idea how long he had been moving like this, on his knees or dragging himself along on his belly in the darkness. He had given up all hope of ever finding the shalwars. What bothered him more and more was the heat. It was like moving around in the attic of a house with a tin roof on a very hot afternoon. He felt the scorching air in his nostrils, and the things he touched seemed to be getting hotter and hotter. His whole body was dripping wet, and he had to stop from time to time to rest. When he did he would stretch out as far as he could, extending his legs and arms like a cross, pressing his face to the carpet, breathing deeply but jerkily and with difficulty.

Once he thought he had dozed off and was awakened by an unexpected breeze, as if a window had been opened somewhere, letting in the cool of night. But he understood immediately that it was something else, something different from anything he was familiar with, and for a moment he remained petrified, feeling how the sweat on his back grew cold. He couldn't remember what happened after that. He let out a yell and was startled by it himself. When he next became aware of his actions, he found himself running around madly in the dark, colliding with screens, overturning mirrors and all sorts of small objects scattered over the carpet in a curious fashion, stumbling and falling repeatedly, but getting up immediately and taking to flight once more. He caught himself jumping over small chests and avoiding the mirrors and screens; and then he realized that he had reached a region of semidarkness, where he could begin to make out the shapes of things. At the end of the corridor there seemed to be a window, unusually high in the wall, through which was coming the light of a summer twilight. When he entered the corridor the heat became unbearable. He had to stop to catch his breath, and with the back of his hand he wiped the sweat from his forehead and cheeks. He heard his heart beating as if it would burst.

Before reaching the window he stopped again, frightened. He could hear voices, laughter, and the sound of chairs being dragged across the floor, as if a whole group had got up from the table and were coming toward him. At that moment he saw that he was naked, thinner than he had ever been. His bones were plainly visible under his skin, and yet his belly was swollen and hanging down. He had never seen himself like this before. He had no time to turn back. He reached out, grabbed a curtain, and started pulling on it. The curtain seemed about to give. Bracing his feet against the wall, he leaned back with all his weight. But then something unexpected happened. He began to feel the curtain pulling him to itself with ever-increasing force, so that a few moments later he found himself pressed to the wall; and although he tried to free himself, letting go of the curtain, he was unsuccessful, and before long he felt himself all wrapped up, squeezed from all sides, as if he had been tied up and stuffed into a bag. Once again it was dark and very hot, and Gavrilescu realized that he couldn't hold out very long, that he would smother. He tried to scream, but his throat was dry and wooden, and the sounds that came out seemed to be muffled in thick felt.

. . .

He heard a voice that he thought he recognized.

"Go on, sir, tell me more."

"What more can I tell you?" he said in a low voice. "I've told you everything. There's nothing more to tell. Elsa and I came to Bucureşti. We were both penniless. I started giving piano lessons."

He raised his head from the pillow a little and saw the old woman. She was sitting at the little table with the coffeepot in her hand and was about to fill the cups again.

"No, thank you, I won't drink any more," he said, raising his arm. "I've drunk enough coffee. I'm afraid I won't sleep tonight."

The old woman filled her cup, then set the pot on a corner of the table.

"Tell me more," she insisted. "What else did you do? What else happened?"

Gavrilescu remained lost in thought for some time, fanning himself with his hat.

"Then we began to play hide-and-seek," he said all at once, in a changed and rather stern voice. "Of course, they didn't know whom they were dealing with. I'm a serious-minded person, I'm an artist and a piano teacher. I came here out of sheer curiosity. I'm always interested in new, unfamiliar things. I said to myself, 'Gavrilescu, here's an opportunity to broaden your experience.' I didn't know that it would involve silly, childish games. Just imagine, suddenly I saw that I was naked, and I heard voices; I was sure that the very next moment . . . You know what I mean."

The old woman nodded her head and took a leisurely sip of coffee.

"What a time we had looking for your hat," she said. "The girls turned the cottage upside down before they could find it."

"Yes, I admit it was partly my fault," Gavrilescu continued. "I didn't know that if I didn't guess them by daylight, I would have to hunt for them, catch them, and guess them in the dark. No one told me anything. And, let me repeat, when I saw that I was naked, and when I felt the curtain wrap itself around me like a shroud—I give you my word of honor, it was like a shroud."

"What a time we had getting you dressed again!" said the old woman. "You just didn't want to let us dress you."

"I tell you, that curtain was like a shroud, it squeezed me from all sides, it enveloped me and squeezed me until I could no longer breathe. And was it hot!" he exclaimed, fanning himself still harder with his hat. "It's a wonder I didn't smother!"

"Yes, it was very hot," said the old woman.

At that moment the metallic screech of the streetcar could be heard in the distance. Gavrilescu put his hand to his forehead.

"Oh!" he exclaimed, getting up from the sofa with difficulty. "How time flies. We've been chatting, and what with one thing and another, I forgot I have to go to Strada Preoteselor. Just imagine, I forgot the portfolio with my music. I was saying to myself after lunch today, 'Gavrilescu, watch out. I'm afraid . . . I'm afraid you . . .' Well, I was telling myself something of the sort, but I don't quite remember what."

He started toward the door, but after a few steps he turned around, bowed slightly from the shoulders, and waved his hat.

"A pleasure to have met you," he said.

Outside in the yard he had an unpleasant surprise. Although the sun had set, it was hotter than it had been in the middle of the afternoon. Gavrilescu took off his jacket and put it over his shoulder. He crossed the yard and went out the gate, fanning himself with his hat all the while. Once he was outside the tree-shaded wall he was again overwhelmed by the burning heat of the pavement and the odor of dust and melted asphalt. He walked dejectedly, with drooping shoulders, staring straight ahead of him. There was no one waiting at the streetcar stop. When he heard the car approaching, he raised his arm and signaled it to stop.

The car was almost empty, and all the windows were open. He sat down across from a young man in shirt sleeves, and as he saw the conductor approaching, he began looking for his wallet. He found it more quickly than he expected.

"It's unheard of!" he exclaimed. "I give you my word of honor that it's worse than in Arabia. If you've ever heard of Colonel Lawrence . . ."

The young man smiled absentmindedly, then turned his face toward the window.

"Can you tell me what time it is?" Gavrilescu asked the conductor.

"Five minutes after eight."

"What rotten luck! They'll be eating dinner when I get there. They'll think I came this late on purpose, so they would be eating dinner. You understand, I wouldn't want them to think that I . . . You understand what I mean. And then, if I tell them where I've been, Mrs. Voitinovici is very curious and will keep me there till midnight to tell her all about it."

The conductor had been watching him with a smile; now he winked at the young man.

"Tell her you've been to the gypsy girls', and you'll see, she won't ask you anything more."

"Oh, no, out of the question. I know her well. She's a very curious woman. Better I don't say anything."

At the next stop a number of young couples got on, and Gavrilescu moved closer to them so that he could listen to their conversation better. When he saw a chance to join in, he raised his arm a little.

"If you'll allow me, I must contradict you. I, unfortunately for me, am a piano teacher, but that's not what I was made for . . ."

"Strada Preoteselor," he heard the conductor announce, and getting up suddenly, he waved and walked quickly down the aisle.

He set off slowly, fanning himself with his hat. In front of No. 18 he stopped, straightened his necktie, ran his hand over his hair, and went in. He climbed the stairs to the first floor slowly, then rang the bell hard. A few moments later he was joined by the young man from the streetcar.

"What a coincidence!" exclaimed Gavrilescu, when he saw the young man stop beside him.

The door opened suddenly, and on the threshold appeared a woman, still young, but with a pale and withered face. She was wearing a kitchen apron and in her left hand she had a pot of mustard. Seeing Gavrilescu, she frowned.

"What can I do for you?" she asked.

"I forgot my portfolio," Gavrilescu began nervously. "I got to talking and I forgot it. I had business in town and couldn't come any earlier."

"I don't understand. What sort of portfolio?"

"If you're eating dinner, I don't want to disturb you," continued Gavrilescu hurriedly. "I know where I left it. It's right next to the piano."

He made a move to enter, but the woman didn't budge from the doorway.

"Who is it you're looking for, sir?"

"For Mrs. Voitinovici. I'm Gavrilescu, Otilia's piano teacher. I don't think I've had the pleasure of meeting you," he added politely.

"You've got the wrong address," said the woman. "This is No. 18."

"Allow me," Gavrilescu began again, with a smile. "I've known this apartment for five years. I might almost say I'm one of the family. I come here three times a week."

The young man had been leaning against the wall, listening to the conversation.

"What did you say her name is?" he asked.

"Mrs. Voitinovici. She's Otilia's aunt. Otilia Pandele."

"She doesn't live here," the young man interrupted him. "This is where *we* live, the Georgescus. This woman before you is my father's wife, née Petrescu."

"Please be polite," said the woman. "And don't bring all kinds of people home with you."

With that she turned her back and disappeared down the hall.

"I beg your pardon for this scene," said the young man, trying to smile. "She's my father's third wife, and she bears on her shoulders all the mistakes of the earlier marriages: five boys and a girl."

Gavrilescu was listening to him in embarrassment, fanning himself with his hat.

"I'm sorry," he began, "I'm very sorry. I didn't mean to make her angry. Of course it *is* a rather inconvenient time. It's dinnertime. But you see, tomorrow morning I have a lesson at Dealul Spirei.* I need my portfolio. I've got Czerny II and III in it. They're my scores, with my own interpretations noted in the margins. That's why I always carry them with me."

The young man continued to look at him with a smile. "I'm afraid I didn't make myself clear," he said. "What I'm

---

*"Switchback Hill."—TRANSLATOR'S NOTE.

trying to tell you is that this is where *we* live, the Georgescu family. We've been here four years."

"Impossible!" exclaimed Gavrilescu. "I was here just a few hours ago and gave Otilia her lesson from two to three. And then I got to talking with Mrs. Voitinovici."

"At Strada Preoteselor 18, first floor?" asked the young man in surprise, with an amused smile.

"Precisely. I know the house very well. I can tell you where the piano is. I'll take you there with my eyes closed. It's in the parlor, next to the window."

"We have no piano," said the young man. "Try another floor. Though, I can tell you, you won't find her on the second floor either. That's were Captain Zamfir and his family live. Try the third floor. I'm very sorry," he added, seeing that Gavrilescu was listening to him with alarm and fanning himself with his hat more and more agitatedly. "I really wish there was an Otilia in this house."

Gavrilescu hesitated, staring at him fixedly.

"Thank you," he said finally. "I *will* try the third floor. But I give you my word of honor that at three or maybe quarter past three I was *here*," and he pointed doggedly to the hall.

He began climbing the stairs, breathing heavily. When he reached the third floor, he spent a long time mopping his face wth one of his handkerchiefs, then rang the bell. He heard a child's steps, and shortly the door was opened by a little boy perhaps five or six years old.

"Oh!" exclaimed Gavrilescu. "I'm afraid I've got the wrong floor. I was looking for Mrs. Voitinovici."

Then a young woman appeared at the door and greeted him with a smile.

"Mrs. Voitinovici used to live on the first floor," she said, "but she moved, she went off to the country."

"Did she move away very long ago?"

"Oh, yes, long ago. It will be eight years this fall. She left right after Otilia got married."

Gavrilescu put his hand to his forehead and began to rub

it. Then he tried to catch her eye and smiled at her as pleasantly as he was able.

"I think you must be mistaken," he began. "It's Otilia Pandele I'm talking about, in the sixth class at the lyceum, Mrs. Voitinovici's niece."

"I knew them both quite well," said the woman. "When we first moved here, Otilia had just become engaged. You know, first there was that business with the major. Mrs. Voitinovici wouldn't give her consent, and she was right, the difference in age was too great. Otilia was still a girl, not yet nineteen. Fortunately she met Francu, Francu the engineer. You must have heard of him."

"Francu the engineer?" Gavrilescu repeated. "Francu?"

"Yes. The inventor. He's been written up in the newspapers."

"Francu the inventor," Gavrilescu repeated dreamily. "How strange . . ."

Then he extended his hand, stroked the little boy on the head, and bowing slightly from the waist he said:

"Please excuse me. I must have gotten the wrong floor."

The young man was waiting for him, leaning against the wall and smoking.

"Did you find out anything?" he asked.

"The lady upstairs claims she got married, but I assure you there's something wrong somewhere. Otilia isn't yet seventeen and she's in the sixth class at the lyceum. I had a long conversation with Mrs. Voitinovici today, and we talked about all sorts of things, but she never said a word about it."

"That's strange."

"Yes, it's very strange," said Gavrilescu, growing bolder. "And for that reason, I tell you, I don't believe a word of it. I give you my word of honor . . . But then, what's the use? There's something wrong somewhere. I'll just have to come back tomorrow morning."

And after saying good-by, he started down the stairs with a resolute air.

"Gavrilescu," he murmured, once he had reached the street, "watch out, you're getting decrepit. You're starting to lose your memory. You're getting the addresses all mixed up." He saw the streetcar coming and began walking faster. No sooner did he sit down by an open window than he began to feel a slight breeze.

"At last!" he exclaimed, addressing the woman across from him. "I think, I think that . . ."

But then he realized that he didn't know how to go on with his sentence, and he smiled with an embarrassed air.

"Yes," he began again after a short pause. "I was talking with a friend of mine not long ago. I think . . . I think I must have been in Arabia. Colonel Lawrence—perhaps you've heard of him."

The woman continued to look out of the window.

"Now, in another hour or two," Gavrilescu started again, "night will fall too. Darkness, I mean. The cool of night. At last! We'll be able to breathe again."

The conductor had stopped in front of him and was waiting there. Gavrilescu began rummaging through his pockets.

"After midnight we'll be able to breathe again," he said, addressing the conductor. "What a long day!" he added, a little nervously, since he hadn't managed to find his wallet. "So many things have happened! . . . Ah, at last!" he exclaimed, and opening his wallet quickly, he handed over a hundred-lei bill.

"This isn't good anymore," said the conductor, handing him back the bill. "You'll have to change it at the bank."

"But what's wrong with it?" asked Gavrilescu in surprise, turning the bill over and over in his fingers.

"They were withdrawn from circulation a year ago. You'll have to change it at the bank."

"How strange!" said Gavrilescu, examining the bill very carefully. "It was good this morning. And they accept them at the gypsy girls'. I had three more just like this one, and they took them all at the gypsy girls'."

The woman paled slightly, and getting up ostentatiously went and sat down at the other end of the car.

"You shouldn't have mentioned the gypsy girls in front of a lady," said the conductor reproachfully.

"Everybody talks about them," Gavrilescu said defensively. "I ride this streetcar three times a week, and I give you my word of honor . . ."

"Yes, it's true," a passenger broke in. "We all talk about them, only not in front of ladies. It's a question of proper behavior. Especially now that the place is going to be illuminated. Oh, yes, and even the city government has given them permission: the garden is going to be illuminated. I am, may I say, a man without any prejudices, but illumination at the gypsy girls' I consider an outrage."

"How strange," remarked Gavrilescu. "I haven't heard anything about it."

"It's been in all the newspapers," put in another passenger. "It's a scandal!" he exclaimed, raising his voice. "It's a crime!"

Several people turned their heads, and under their reproachful gaze Gavrilescu lowered his eyes.

"Keep looking, perhaps you have some other money," said the conductor. "If not, you'll have to get off at the next stop."

Blushing and not daring to raise his eyes, Gavrilescu began searching in his pockets some more. Fortunately his change purse was right on top, among the handkerchiefs. Gavrilescu counted out a few coins and handed them to him.

"You've given me five lei," said the conductor, showing him the coins in his hand.

"Yes, I'm getting off at Vama Poştei."*

"I don't care where you're getting off, the ticket costs ten lei. Where in the world have you been keeping yourself?" added the conductor in a stern voice.

*"Postal Toll House."—TRANSLATOR'S NOTE.

"I live in Bucureşti," said Gavrilescu, proudly raising his eyes, "and I ride on the streetcar three or four times a day, and I've been doing this for years on end, and I've always paid five lei."

Nearly everyone on the car was now listening to the conversation with interest. Several passengers moved closer and sat down nearby. The conductor tossed the coins in his hand several times and then spoke.

"If you won't give me the rest, you'll have to get off at the next stop."

"The fare went up three or four years ago," said someone.

"Five years ago," the conductor corrected him.

"I give you my word of honor," began Gavrilescu pathetically.

"Then get off at the next stop," the conductor interrupted him.

"Better pay the difference," someone advised him, "because it's quite a ways to walk from here to Vama Poştei."

Gavrilescu looked in his purse and gave the conductor five lei more.

"Strange things are happening in this country," he muttered after the conductor had gone. "Decisions are made overnight. In twenty-four hours. More precisely, in six hours. I give you my word of honor. . . But then, what's the use? I've had a terrible day. And the worst thing about it is that we can't live without the streetcar. At least *I* can't. The life I lead obliges me to ride the streetcar three or four times a day. And at that, one piano lesson is only a hundred lei. One hundred-lei bill like this. And now even this bill isn't good anymore. I have to go and get it changed at the bank."

"Give it to me," said an elderly gentleman. "I'll change it at the office tomorrow."

He took a bill out of his wallet and handed it to him. Gavrilescu took it gingerly and examined it closely.

"It's beautiful," he said, "How long ago did they put them into circulation?"

Several passengers exchanged glances, smiling.

"About three years ago," said one.

"It's strange that I've never seen one till now. Of course, I'm a bit absentminded. I have the soul of an artist."

He put the bill in his wallet, then let his glance stray out of the window.

"Night has fallen," he said. "At last!"

He suddenly felt worn out and weary, and resting his head in his hand, he closed his eyes. He remained like that all the way to Vama Poştei.

. . .

He had tried in vain to unlock the door with his key, and then had pushed the bell button for a long time; after knocking several times on the dining room windows as loudly as he could, he went back to the front door and began beating on it with his fist. Soon, at the open window of a neighboring house, there appeared in the darkness a man in a nightshirt, who called out hoarsely:

"What's all the commotion, man? What's got into you?"

"Excuse me," said Gavrilescu. "I don't know what's happened to my wife. She doesn't answer the door. And my key doesn't work either, so I can't get into the house."

"But what do you want to get in for? Who are you?"

Gavrilescu turned toward the window and introduced himself.

"Although we're neighbors," he began, "I don't believe I've had the pleasure of meeting you. My name is Gavrilescu and I live here with my wife, Elsa."

"You must have the wrong address. That's where *Dl* Stănescu lives. And he's not home, he's gone to the shore."

"Allow me," Gavrilescu interrupted him. "I'm sorry to contradict you, but I think you've got it all wrong. Elsa and I live here, No. 101. We've been here four years."

"Cut it out, gentlemen, we can't sleep!" someone called out. "Good God!"

"He claims he lives in *Dl* Stănescu's house."

"I don't *claim*," Garvrilescu protested. "This is my house, and I won't allow anyone to . . . But above all I want to find out where Elsa is, what's happened to her."

"Inquire at the police station," put in someone on the next floor.

"Why the police station? What's happened?" he cried in agitation. "Do you know something?"

"No, I don't know anything, but I want to sleep. And if you're going to stand there all night chatting . . ."

"Allow me," said Gavrilescu. "I'm sleepy too; in fact, I may say I'm all worn out. I've had a terrible day. And the heat's been as bad as in Arabia . . . But I don't understand what's happened to Elsa; why doesn't she answer the door? Perhaps she felt sick and fainted."

And turning back to the door of No. 101, he started beating on it with his fist again, louder and louder.

"I told you he's not at home, sir, didn't I? *Dl* Stănescu has gone to the shore."

"Call the police!" he heard a woman cry in a shrill voice. "Call the police at once!"

Gavrilescu stopped instantly and leaned against the door, breathing heavily. Suddenly he felt very weary, and he sat down on the steps and leaned his head in his hands. "Gavrilescu," he murmured, "watch out, something very serious has happened, and they don't want to tell you. Get hold of yourself, try to remember."

"Mme. Trandafir!"* he exclaimed. "Why didn't I think of her before? Mme. Trandafir!" he called, standing up and turning toward the house across the street. "Mme. Trandafir!"

---

*The name means "Rose."—TRANSLATOR'S NOTE.

Someone who had stayed at the window said in a quieter voice, "Let her sleep, poor woman."

"It's quite urgent!"

"Let her sleep, God rest her soul, she died long ago."

"Impossible," said Gavrilescu, "I talked with her this morning."

"You must be confusing her with her sister, Ecaterina. Mme. Trandafir died five years ago."

Gavrilescu stood there a moment stupefied, then put his hands in his pockets and took out a number of handkerchiefs.

"How strange," he finally murmured.

He turned away slowly, and going up the three steps at No. 101, picked up his hat and put it on his head. He tried the door once more, then went back down the steps and started walking away, at a loss what to do now. He walked slowly, thinking of nothing, and mopping his forehead mechanically with a handkerchief. The tavern on the corner was still open, and after walking past it irresolutely, he decided to go in.

"We're only serving by the glass now," said the waiter. "We close at two."

"At two?" asked Gavrilescu in surprise. "What time is it now?"

"It's two. In fact, it's after two."

"It's terribly late," Gavrilescu murmured, as if to himself.

Going up to the counter, he thought the tavern keeper's face looked familiar, and his heart began to beat faster.

"Aren't you Mr. Costică?" he asked.

"Yes, I am," replied the tavern keeper, looking at him closely. "Don't I know you?" he added after a pause.

"I think, I think that . . .," began Gavrilescu, but then he lost the train of his thought and fell silent, with an embarrassed smile on his face. "I used to come around here a long time ago," he began again. "I had friends here. Mme. Trandafir."

"Yes, God rest her soul."

"Mme. Gavrilescu, Elsa."

"Oh, yes, what a time she had," the tavern keeper interrupted. "To this very day no one knows what happened. The police searched for him for several months but were never able to find any trace of him, dead or alive. It was as if he'd been swallowed up by the earth. Poor Mme. Elsa, she waited and waited for him, and then finally went back to her family, in Germany. She sold everything she had and left. They didn't have much, they were penniless. I myself had some thought of buying their piano."

"So she left for Germany," said Gavrilescu pensively. "How long ago did she leave?"

"A long time ago. A few months after Gavrilescu's disappearance. In the fall it will be twelve years. It was all written up in the papers."

"How strange," murmured Gavrilescu, starting to fan himself with his hat. "And what if I should tell you . . . if I should tell you that this morning—and I give you my word of honor that I'm not exaggerating—this very morning I was talking to her. And what's more, we had lunch together. I can even tell you what we had to eat."

"Then she must have come back," said the tavern keeper, looking at him in perplexity.

"No, she hasn't come back. She never left. There's something very wrong somewhere. Right now I'm quite tired, but tomorrow morning I'll find out what it's all about."

He bowed slightly and left.

. . .

He walked slowly, his hat in one hand and a handkerchief in the other, stopping to rest a while at every bench. It was a clear night, with no moon, and the coolness of the gardens was beginning to pour out into the streets. After some time a one-horse cab drove up beside him.

"Where are you going, sir?" asked the cab driver.

"To the gypsy girls', " replied Gavrilescu.

"Then get in. I'll take you there for forty lei," said the cab driver, stopping the cab.

"I'm sorry, but I haven't got much money. All I have left is a hundred lei and a little change. And I'll need a hundred to get in at the gypsy girls'."

"It'll take more than that," said the cab driver with a laugh. "A hundred lei won't do it."

"That's all I paid this afternoon. Good night," he added, setting off once more.

But the cab kept right with him, at a walk.

"That's the Queen of the Night," said the cab driver, taking a deep breath. "It's coming from the General's garden. That's why I like to drive this way at night. Whether I have passengers or not, I drive this way every night. I'm awfully fond of flowers."

"You have the soul of an artist," said Gavrilescu with a smile.

With that he sat down on a bench and waved him good-by. But the cab driver stopped the cab suddenly and pulled up alongside him, right next to the bench. He took out his tobacco box and began rolling a cigarette.

"I love flowers," he said. "Horses and flowers. When I was young I drove a hearse. And what a beauty! Six horses with black trappings and gold fittings, and flowers, flowers, masses of flowers! Alas, youth is past and they're all gone. I've grown old; I've become a night cab driver, with only one horse."

He lit his cigarette and took a long pull at it.

"Well now, you're going to the gypsy girls'," he said finally.

"Yes, it's a personal matter," Gavrilescu hastened to explain. "I was there this afternoon and somehow got involved in a terrible mix-up."

"Ah, the gypsy girls!" said the cab driver sadly. "If it wasn't for the gypsy girls," he added, lowering his voice. "If it wasn't for . . ."

"Yes," said Gavrilescu, "everybody talks about them. On the streetcar, I mean. When the streetcar goes past their garden, everybody talks about the gypsy girls."

He got up from the bench and set off once again, the cab staying right with him at a walk.

"Let's go this way," said the cab driver, pointing with his whip to an alley. "It's a shortcut. And this way we go past a church. The Queen of the Night is in bloom there too. Of course, it's not as fine as at the General's, but I don't think you'll be sorry."

"You have the soul of an artist," said Gavrilescu dreamily.

In front of the church they both stopped to breathe in the perfume from the flowers.

"I think there's something else there besides the Queen of the Night," said Gavrilescu.

"Oh, there are all kinds of flowers. If there was a funeral here today, lots of flowers were left. And now, toward morning, all these flower scents are freshening up again. I often used to come here with the hearse. How lovely it all was!"

He whistled to his horse and set off again at the same time as Gavrilescu.

"We don't have much farther to go now," he said. "Why don't you get in?"

"I'm sorry, but I don't have any money."

"Just give me some of your change. Get in."

Gavrilescu hesitated a couple of moments, then, with an effort, got in. But as soon as the cab started up, he put his head down on the cushion and fell asleep.

"It was lovely," began the cab driver. "It was a rich church, and none but the best people. Ah, youth!"

He turned his head; seeing Gavrilescu asleep, he began to whistle softly, and the horse began to trot.

. . .

"Here we are," he cried, climbing down from the box. "But the gates are closed."

He began to shake Gavrilescu, who awoke with a start.

"The gates are closed," the cab driver repeated. "You'll have to ring."

Gavrilescu picked up his hat, straightened his tie, and got out. Then he began to look for his change purse.

"Don't bother to look for it," said the cab driver. "You can give it to me some other time. I've got to wait here anyway," he added. "At this time of day, if I'm to get a passenger at all, this is where I'll find him."

Gavrilescu waved to the cab driver with his hat, then went up to the gate, found the bell, and pushed the button. The gate opened instantly; Gavrilescu entered the yard and headed toward the grove. A feeble light could still be seen at one of the windows. He knocked on the door timidly; seeing that no one came to answer, he opened the door and went in. The old woman had fallen asleep with her head on the little table.

"It's me, Gavrilescu," he said, tapping her on the shoulder. "You played some monstrous tricks on me," he added, seeing that she was waking up and starting to yawn.

"It's late," said the old woman, rubbing her eyes. "There's no one here."

But then, taking a long look at him, she recognized him and smiled.

"Oh, it's you again, the musician. The German girl might still be here. She never sleeps."

Gavrilescu felt his heart beat faster, and he began to tremble slightly.

"The German girl?" he repeated.

"A hundred lei," said the old woman.

Gavrilescu began looking for his wallet, but his hands were trembling more and more, and when at last he found it, among the handkerchiefs, he dropped it on the floor.

"Excuse me," he said, bending down with difficulty to pick it up. "I'm all worn out. I've had a terrible day."

The old woman took the hundred-lei bill, got up from her

stool, and going to the door, waved her arm toward the big house.

"Now be careful you don't get lost," she told him. "Go straight down the corridor and count seven doors. And when you get to the seventh, knock three times and say: 'It's me, the old woman sent me.'"

Then she put her hand to her mouth to stifle a yawn, and closed the door after him. Scarcely daring to breathe, Gavrilescu walked slowly toward the building, which gleamed with a silvery light under the stars. He mounted the marble steps, opened the door, and paused a moment in indecision. In front of him stretched a feebly-lighted corridor, and Gavrilescu again felt his heart begin to beat wildly, as if about to burst. He began walking along the corridor, excited, counting each door in a loud voice as he passed. But then he found himself counting, "Thirteen, fourteen . . ." and he stopped in confusion. "Gavrilescu," he murmured, "watch out, you've gotten all mixed up again. Not thirteen, not fourteen, but seven. That's what the old woman said, to count seven doors."

He started to go back to begin counting all over again, but after a few steps he was overcome by exhaustion. Stopping at the first door he came to, he knocked three times and went in. The room was large but simple, and meagerly furnished. At the window he could see the silhouette of a young woman looking out into the garden.

"Excuse me," Gavrilescu began, with some difficulty. "I made a mistake counting the doors."

The figure left the window and came toward him with soft steps, and suddenly he recalled a forgotten perfume.

"Hildegard!" he exclaimed, dropping his hat.

"I've been waiting for you such a long time!" said the girl, coming closer to him. "I looked for you everywhere."

"I went to a beer hall," murmured Gavrilescu. "If I hadn't gone to the beer hall with her, nothing would have happened. Or if I'd had any money on me . . . But as it was, *she* paid—Elsa paid—and, you understand, I felt obliged . . . And now it's late, isn't it? It's very late."

"What does that matter now?" asked the girl. "Come on, let's go!"

"But I don't even have a house anymore, I don't have anything. I've had a terrible day. I stopped to chat with Mrs. Voitinovici and I forgot the portfolio with my scores."

"You always were absentminded," the girl interrupted him. "Let's go."

"But where? Where?" asked Gavrilescu, trying to shout. "Somebody has moved into my house. I forget his name, but it's somebody I don't know. And he's not even at home so that I can explain it all to him. He's gone to the shore."

"Come with me," said the girl, taking his hand and pulling him gently toward the corridor.

"But I don't even have any money," continued Gavrilescu in a low voice. "Right now when they've changed the currency and the streetcar fare has gone up!"

"You're just the same as ever," said the girl, starting to laugh. "You're afraid."

"And nobody's left of all my acquaintances," continued Gavrilescu. "Everybody's at the shore. And Mrs. Voitinovici, from whom I could have borrowed something, they say she's moved to the country . . . Oh, my hat!" he exclaimed, and was about to go back to get it.

"Leave it there," replied the girl. "You won't need it any more now."

"You never can tell, you never can tell," Gavrilescu insisted, trying desperately to free his hand from the girl's grasp. "It's a very good hat, and almost new."

"Can it be true?" asked the girl in amazement. "You still don't understand? You don't understand what's happened to you, now, a short while ago, a very short while ago? Is it true that you don't understand?"

Gavrilescu looked deep into her eyes, then heaved a sigh.

"I'm all worn out," he said. "Forgive me. I've had a terrible day . . . But now I think I'm starting to feel better."

The girl pulled him gently along after her. They crossed the yard and went out without even opening the gate. The cab driver was waiting for them, dozing, he saw; and the girl pulled him ever so gently into the cab with her.

"But I swear," began Gavrilescu in a whisper, "I give you my word of honor that I haven't got a cent."

"Where to, lady?" asked the cab driver. "And how do you want me to drive? At a walk, or faster?"

"Drive us to the woods, and go the longest way," said the girl. "And drive slowly. We're in no hurry."

"Ah, youth!" said the cab driver, whistling softly to his horse.

She was holding his hand between her hands, leaning back with her head on the cushion, looking at the sky. Gavrilescu gazed at her intently, lost in thought.

"Hildegard," he began finally. "Something's happening to me, and I don't quite understand what. If I hadn't heard you speak to the cab driver, I would think I was dreaming."

The girl turned her head toward him and smiled.

"We're all dreaming," she said. "That's how it begins. As if in a dream . . ."